Praise

The Gift of Nine Lives is a sweet, sly, completely irresistible re-imagining of the story of creation. This feline Bible unlocks the mysteries and wonders of the magical creatures who warm our hearths and our hearts. It is a wonderful gift for any cat-lover, clarifying, as it does, the lives of the Divine's true crown of creation: cats!

—Kathy McCoy, Ph.D.,
Author of *Purr Therapy: What Timmy and Marina Taught Me About Life, Love and Loss*

I must admit to not knowing Old Testament stories very well. So I was more tuned in to the Good Mews of the New Testament. I loved the tongue-in-cheek humor throughout! A great Christmas book for cat lovers who are looking for new twists to old stories.

—Marge Tansley, beloved companion of Cooper, who has dedicated his feline life to her

The Gift of Nine Lives is a fanciful inventive tale for cat lovers. It's a fantasy bible and imaginative history for the feline world

—Rian Hartdegen, retired AMT with a B.S. in Animal Science, who has been privileged to share the last fifteen years with Tux, Julie, and Ghost: three quite entertaining and endearing felines.

The Gift of Nine Lives

Book One of the Bastet-Net Cat Fantasy Series

Written by Dee Ready

Illustrated by Judy King-Rieniets

HODOS·BOOKS

Hodos·Books
Independence, Missouri

The Gift of Nine Lives

First Edition
Text and Illustrations © 2018 by Dee Ready
Cover by Judy King-Rieniets and Sally Brewer

ISBN-13: 978-1-948793-06-3

Published by Hodos·Books
Independence, Missouri
10 9 8 7 6 5 4 3 2

© 2018 Dee Ready. All rights reserved. Printed in the U.S.A.
Material in this book may not be reproduced in whole or in part
in any form or format without special permission from the
publisher, Hodos·Books.

Dedication

To Judy,

whose ideas sparked the first chapter of this fantasy,
whose continued interest kept me writing,
and whose art captured
the land and costumes of the Nile
and the regal beauty of felines.

Contents

Dedication v

Contents vii

Epigraph...ix

Editor's Forepurr..xi

Chapter 1 Bastet-Net Creates a Universe.................1

Chapter 2 Mosi Teaches Her Kits.............................7

Chapter 3 Felines Praise Bastet-Net......................13

Chapter 4 Recalcitrant Rebels Impoverish Siti.........19

Chapter 5 Lady Siti Patiently Waits.......................25

Chapter 6 Bastet-Net Yowls through Kosey.............33

Chapter 7 Runihura Plots Feline Destruction..........39

Chapter 8 Mafuane Sails to Britain.......................45

Chapter 9 Osaze Fights for Freedom.....................53

Chapter 10 A Canine Seeks Détente......................61

Chapter 11 Tabia Experiences a Dream..................69

Chapter 12 Bastet-Net Purrs within Tabia..............75

Chapter 13 A Judge Silences Tabia........................83

Chapter 14 Tabia's Companions Depart Thebes.......89

Chapter 15 Tabia's Companions Travel Far and Wide............95

Chapter 16 Omar Encounters Mystery.................................101

Chapter 17 Omar Yowls the Good Mews 107

Epigraph

Wolf shall live at peace with lamb,
leopard take its ease with kid;
calf and lion and sheep in one dwelling place,
with a little child to lead them!
Cattle and bears all at pasture,
their young ones lying down together,
lion eating straw like ox.

Isaiah 11:6-7
The Knox Translation of the Holy Bible

Editor's Forepurr

Eliza Calico, head of the feline history department at Mau University in Minneapolis, Minnesota, translated this edition of *The Gift of Nine Lives*. The feline Bible was originally pawed by a clowder of scribes more than two millennia ago.

Calico received her undergraduate degree in feline history and mythology at the University of Catnapping in Lancing, Michigan. She obtained her master's and doctorate at the University of Litter Box in San Francisco, California. Having completed these two degrees, she settled in the former home of a feline lumberjack in Stillwater, Minnesota.

There she began a serious study of the Coptic language of ancient Egypt. During a particularly long blizzard in January 2016, Calico decided to translate the early feline scriptures—originally written in Coptic—into modern feline, using the idioms of our time.

It is this translation you now have in paw. *The Gift of Nine Lives* contains the ancient stories of our race. May it lead you to great heights of yowling!

JUDY KING-RIENIETS 2013

Chapter 1
Bastet-Net Creates a Universe

Before moon rose and sun set, Bastet-Net, the great god of cats, slept . . . and dreamed. In her dream, she bowed her sleek head over an empty bowl. Yawning, she breathed sky. It arced the hollow bowl from rim to rim.

Then Bastet-Net hissed. Thunder rumbled. Lightning skittered azure sky. Raindrops filled the bowl. The great god of cats lowered her head and drank deep of her creation.

Twitching her whiskers, she howled. Flames sparked a fiery ball, which lit the abyss in which the bowl of creation floated. Bastet-Net called the flaming ball *sun*. When she blinked, crescent moon rose in her eyes to guide night to dawn, while sun led day to dusk. Always then, the great god of cats cradled sun and moon in her almond eyes.

As she dreamed, Bastet-Net yowled. Dust whirled into orb. Swiping the ball with her right paw, she sent it soaring out into boundless space to circle sun. The great god of cats called the dust ball *earth*.

Rain, falling softly on earth, gathered itself into river and ocean. When Bastet-Net swished her tail, silvered fish cavorted in the deep. As the great god of cats miaowed, vole tunneled beneath the loam of earth. Mouse nestled among marsh grass. Bird ascended sky.

1

Bastet-Net stretched. Licking a paw, she groomed her soft fur, bemused by her own perfection. Contentedly, the great god of cats curled her tail round herself and purred.

In the sweetness of that purr, cat was born. She wore a silver coat, spotted with midnight soot. Bastet-Net called her Mosi for she was the first born of all felines—the crown of creation.

Dreaming then, the great god of cats wailed. In the agony of that wail, first-born of all canines came to be. Flanks quivering, he barked. Eager to serve, dog sniffed the dust of earth.

As the great god of cats slumbered, Mosi—the delight of Bastet-Net—groomed her whiskers. Then she, too, slept, dreaming her own sweet dream of mice and vole, fish and bird. Wailing, she dreamed of dog. In her dream, first cat fought him.

With claw and tooth, she sent dog yelping into the calamity of mange. In her dream, Mosi smiled, savoring the wonder of herself.

*   *   *

Mosi slept so often and so long that Bastet-Net wearied of waiting for her to wake. Finally, she nudged first cat. Once and then again. When Mosi ignored this summons, Bastet-Net thumped her on her black nose.

Startled, Mosi woke, mewing remorse at having displeased the great god of cats. Well satisfied, Bastet-Net began to teach her first born.

After learning the stealth of hunt, Mosi discovered every nook and cranny created for her by Bastet-Net. As seven full moons wandered across the sky, first cat grew strong and lean.

Finding her own body eager for young, Mosi beseeched Bastet-Net for a litter. With a final lick from her raspy tongue and a touch of her nose, the great god of cats sent Mosi out into the valley of the great river to prowl.

Seeking her young, first cat roamed the valley of the broad river where Bastet-Net had dreamed her into being. There she smelled the rich silt the Nile carried to the delta. Weaving her way, Mosi stalked the bulrushes of the marsh. Next, she trekked the desert dunes. Daily she searched, but found no kits.

Longing to nuzzle her young, Mosi reproached Bastet-Net.

You bedeck sky with birds.

You fill water with fish.

You tempt me with mice.

Yet you give me no young.

Like You, I am mother.

Listen to my yowl.

Bestow kits on me.

Bastet-Net remained indifferent to first cat's rebuke. Who was this creature to scold the great god of cats?

Mosi sulked. Observing her peevishness, Bastet-Net began to grin. Thunder clapped. Lightning split the sky. As rain pelted the fur of first cat, Mosi yowled indignation.

Throughout night and into day, rain fell. Rivulets inched toward the shrub where first cat crouched. When mud dirtied her pads, Mosi relinquished contentiousness and implored Bastet-Net to listen to her plea.

> *O Great God of Cats,*
>
> *I beseech You*
>> *with my sweetest purr,*
>> *dream my kits within me,*
>> *so that I might dream them, too.*

With a deep rumble of content, Bastet-Net curled herself into sleep. She dreamed of first male and named him Manu for he was her second-born feline.

As first male sniffed air, Mosi perfumed it with her need for kits while rubbing her head against her side and writhing the ground.

Cautiously, then, Manu approached.

With sharp claws, Mosi swiped his side. "No farther!" she commanded.

Cowed, first male retreated.

As Mosi looked away in disgust, Manu chirped his own dream. It settled over first cat so that she ceased to watch him approach. It was then he bred her before bounding away. Aggrieved, Mosi watched as her mate disappeared into night.

Feeling her body grow round with kits, Mosi hid within the fissure of a cave. After two waning sickle moons rose, she birthed three kits. Gathering them into the curve of herself, she sang her gratitude to Bastet Net.

Thank You, O Great God of Cats, for my little ones.

Thank You for the night in which I prowl.

Thank You for the day in which I snooze.

Thank You for the wonder of myself.

Thank You, too, for the splendor that is You.

Thank You that I, purring within your purr, am Thou.

We are One.

Once again, Bastet-Net grinned, and mice scurried within the cave. Rising from her litter, Mosi pounced.

Chapter 2
Mosi Teaches Her Kits

Once her kits opened their eyes, Mosi demonstrated for them the fine art of grace. Not for them the lumbering leap or careless crouch. Soon they knew themselves to be beings without equal. For this they thanked Bastet-Net.

After teaching her kits to be captivating, Mosi nudged them into a circle around her to tell them about the great god of cats.

"Many naps ago," she miaowed, "more naps than any of you have slept, Bastet-Net purred nine commands to me. So sweetly did she purr that I've never forgotten them. Now I bequeath these commands to you."

As the kits edged forward to nestle against her warm belly, Mosi yowled each of Bastet-Net's nine commands.

1. *Spray your scent—the gift of Bastet-Net.*

2. *Sniff all scents so as to discover who cowers before you.*

3. *Yowl Bastet-Net's dream of you when greeting stars and moon.*

4. *Diligently practice the refined leap.*

5. *When not napping, yawning, eating, or exploring, groom assiduously.*

6. *Teach your kits to sharpen their claws on whatever is handy.*

7. *Purr your pleasure that all creatures hold you in awe.*

8. *Hunt relentlessly, but always with stealth.*

9. *Remember that you are exceptional because I, Bastet-Net, made you so.*

"We will follow these commands," Mosi's kits promised, "ever and always!"

"Never forget that Bastet-Net made you and you are hers," Mosi counseled her kits. "Praise her! Yowl her praise long and loud throughout dark of night into dawn of day!"

*   *   *

Despite their promise, the kits, as they grew, wearied of thanking the great god of cats. "We are pleasing in all our ways!" they grumbled. "Bastet-Net should be grateful to us! Why do we slink before her?"

Hearing this complaint, Mosi twitched her whiskers. "You speak foolishly!" she warned her kits. Frightened, they cowered before their mother. Once again, she welcomed them to nestle against her.

"My little ones, ever and always I am grateful to the great god of cats. She gave us this land watered by the Nile. She dreamed the span of our life. We are remarkable only because she is."

Mosi began to groom her kits. Between each soothing lick, she miaowed, "We are Bastet-Net's dream. Her purr perfects us."

Content, the kits napped against their mother's side, each within the dream that Bastet-Net herself dreamed. While they slumbered, Mosi purred her thanksgiving.

> *O Great God of Cats,*
> > *thank You for these kits.*
> *Thank You for the mice*
> > *I hunt for them.*
> *Do not forget us,*
> > *O Bastet-Net.*

*   *   *

As years tumbled into past, Mosi and her kits gave birth to a expanding clowder of felines. Before the new kits began to nap each day, Mosi purred them the story of creation. All her descendants learned from Mosi, the first cat, the nine commands of Bastet-Net.

And all of them grieved as Mosi's whiskers grew white and her eyesight dimmed. One day, in the middle of purring a story, her mews stilled to silence. She dozed, her head resting on her outstretched paws.

"She's old," one kit complained to his brothers and sisters. "Why does Bastet-Net let us grow old? Why can't we always be kits?"

Awakening, Mosi twitched her whiskers. Observing her kits' disgruntlement, she taught one final lesson.

"It is now," Mosi purred, "when I am old, that my dream has become that of Bastet-Net's. She has blessed us above all creatures."

"But you can no longer stalk without a limp," one of her sons yowled.

"You snooze instead of hunt," another mewed.

"Your belly hangs. Ribs score your coat," a third complained.

"No matter what delicacy we bring you, you turn away. How is this good, Mother?" one of her daughters miaowed.

"It is good because as I nap, I dream of Bastet-Net. Remembering all she has taught me, I feel gratitude engulf me."

"For what are you thankful?" Mosi's offspring asked.

"For your sleek fur. Your nimble pounce. Your prowl. Your purr. Your fragrant scent. Your tufted ears."

Mosi gazed benignly at her descendants. Content, she purred them her hymn of thanksgiving to Bastet-Net.

I am old now, O Great God of Cats.

Ready to dream with You.

Ready to forego the hunt, the prowl, the stealth.

Ready to gracefully rest within Your dream.

Ready to curve my being into Your purr.

Call me, then, O Bastet-Net.

Hearing this request, the great god of cats enfolded Mosi in harmonious light. It filtered within and about her, over and under her, through and beyond her like mist infusing first dawn.

It was then that the wanderings of Mosi ceased.

She now dreams forever within the purr of Bastet-Net.

Chapter 3
Felines Praise Bastet-Net

Holding fast to the commands Mosi had yowled, her descendants padded north and south, east and west across the valley of the great river. Felines mated and bred other kits.

On whales' broad backs, they sailed beyond the distant isle of Britain.

Astride braying donkeys, they traveled to far-off Babylon.

On yaks, they scaled the snow-capped mountains of Tibet.

Migrating felines prowled woodland and desert, swamp and steppe, prairie and rainforest. Always they miaowed one hymn to Bastet Net.

Bless us, O Great God of Cats.

Give us bird and vole, beast and canine,
   mole and jackal to astound.

Give us crocodile and ibis,
   hippopotamus and cow to amaze.

Give us cricket and ant, beetle and snake to
   enchant.

Bless us, O Great God of Cats.

Give us contentment within a patch of sunlight.

Give us guile within the marrow of our bones.

Give us stealth within the silence of our pad.

Bless us, O Great God of Cats.

Make our ears alert to prey.

Make our nose attuned to scent.

Make our eyes watchful for movement
beneath shrub and brush.

Bless us, O Bastet-Net.

Bless us, for we are feline,

And You, O Blessed One, created us.

*   *   *

Seven years stretched into seventy. Seventy swelled into seven hundred, and felines roamed the arc of earth. Each year, many of them journeyed to the great festival of Bastet-Net to praise her graciousness.

They crowded into boats, yowling delight as the lateen sails carried them up the Nile to the temple of Bastet-Net.

Male cats piped jubilant melodies while kits shook sistrums and mothers clapped their paws. Within all, melody thrummed. Blissfully, they leapt and jumped and sprang upward before Bastet-Net.

As wind captured canvas, the pilgrims skimmed the river, arriving soon at her temple. There, they lauded Bastet-Net's goodness and generosity and mercy.

For five days, they praised her with dance and song.

Together, the joyful throng thanked her for protecting all mothers, for helping them bear their young, for bringing forth milk in their nipples to nurse their kits.

Yowling, the felines thanked Bastet-Net for teaching them how to nurture and train their kits.

*   *   *

Other creatures, too, fancied this festival, for merriment flowed like the Nile's swift current.

Ibis and hawk winged the sky.

Bellowing praise to the great god of cats, hippopotami and crocodiles lifted their snouts toward Sirius.

Canines, too, praised her. As the brightest star in the heavens rose, they proclaimed the glory of Bastet-Net with woof and bark and yelp.

Jubilation captured the spirit of all who entered this holy place. No quarrels or spite, no envy or jealousy rent the hearts of the creatures gathered at the temple. All creatures who reverenced felines rejoiced in the bounty of the great god of cats.

A multitude of creatures barked, bellowed, quaked, gobbled, cooed, and bleated their own songs of praise.

Spelling out Bastet-Net's ancient name, ibis and hawks flew in formation across the sky above the temple.

In their mouths, crocodiles carried marsh flowers to strew before the pilgrims as they entered this hallowed place long dedicated to the great god of cats.

Lean canines ran races around Bastet-Net's temple. The winner of each race won the honor of joining a choir of hounds that barked a canticle in counterpoint to praise Bastet-Net.

Oh, the rapture of those days! The tinkling of the sistrum! The sweet whistle of the reed pipes! The dulcet tones of the lyre!

Every creature gathered there twirled and danced, skipped and leaped in jubilation. During those days, cats—and their fellow creatures—lived in the dream of Bastet-Net.

* * *

As centuries passed, all creatures bowed low before the perfection of cats. And why not? They wore the air of command that distinguished incomparable beings.

Canines built homes for them with a multitude of closets and hidey-holes. The windows they designed featured wide sills on which cats could snooze.

Before the fireplaces, which these same canines had laid brick by brick, the indolent cats could nap away the carefree hours of their days.

The canine slaves furnished their masters' homes with cushions and tapestries fashioned from the silk that oriental caterpillars worked overtime to spin.

Dogs everywhere hauled wood for pillars on which cats could scratch their intricate art.

With bristling tails, foxes brushed dust and dirt from the homes of their feline mistresses and masters.

Wolves opened and closed doors so that cats need never lift a paw to serve themselves.

Beavers sculpted toys for kits; jackals composed melodies to soothe them.

Awaiting the blessed day when cats would devour their plump bodies, birds served their masters in the interim by planting seeds. From these, tall trees grew around each home in which felines lived.

Blasé cats, lounging on the limbs of these trees, purred contentedly when passers-by exclaimed over their beauty. Always cats knew themselves to be amazingly magnificent.

*   *   *

While most felines practiced oppression, some refused to choose the servitude of others and continued to follow the commands of Bastet-Net. Trusting in their own sharp claws to hunt, they stalked their own prey.

"We'll be beholden to no one and nothing!" they proclaimed.

Dressed in tabby, they built their own rickety huts and worked in the marketplace where they sold stones for sharpening claws, sacks of mint for ecstatic play, and brushes for grooming.

Such behavior puzzled those cats served by other creatures.

"Clearly," they complained, "these serfs have no understanding of what is due our superiority."

"How dull-witted these stubborn felines are," others grumbled. "Not like us."

Some felines who enjoyed having servants yowled, "Bastet-Net must daily vomit these unruly cats out of her mouth. And surely out of her dreams. They are nothing but hairballs."

So while a few felines respected other creatures. Most did not . . . and why should they? After all, all creatures everywhere begged cats to rule, for felines knew the sure law of command.

So it was. Cats ruled. And life was good—for cats. And surely, that was all that mattered.

Chapter 4
Recalcitrant Rebels Impoverish Siti

During this time, a well-born feline named Siti dwelt in the delta of the mighty river. The land she owned stretched from the banks of the Nile to the western desert.

Her estate was the finest in Egypt.

In her mines, workers unceasingly chipped copper and gold for her coffers.

Her granaries overflowed with barley and flax.

In her vineyards, clusters of plump grapes awaited the snip of jackals' teeth who stamped them into wine to sell in distant lands.

Siti's palm groves provided sweet fruit for travelers as they trekked trade routes to Syria and beyond.

In her swamps, crocodiles snapped bulrushes.

From them, voles made sheets of papyrus on which ibis scribes penned the sweet history of felines.

From these same bulrushes, monkeys wove baskets and mats, which furnished every home in Egypt.

Her bulrush sandals protected the feet of creatures throughout her homeland and beyond.

Moreover, her workers fashioned seaworthy vessels by binding bulrushes into bundles. Fleets of these feluccas with their lateen sails billowed up and down the great river carrying crops grown on her land.

Her bulrush ropes rigged ships sailing the Great Sea.

In her kilns, workers fashioned bricks for all the finer dwellings of felines.

The oil they pressed from flax, castor beans, and sesame seeds lit homes throughout Egypt.

Counted among her servants were one jackal vintner, three ibis scribes, five canine carpenters, seven crocodile cooks, one pig pool-cleaner, and one feline who lit candles in the shrines. All these creatures dwelt in their own rooms. Each served Lady Siti wholeheartedly.

Within her home, Siti's family reveled in the comfort of her wealth. She enjoyed seven mates, and from seven litters came twenty-seven kits, born of the ancient family of Mau.

Tutors taught each litter of kits melodious yowls and elegant expressions. Scribes demonstrated for them the fine art of scratch and claw.

When each litter's kits matured, their mother—Lady Siti—sent them to school in Athens, Rome, Thebes, or Antioch.

Siti treated her servants with respect. For those who worked the mines, she provided fresh water and roasted perch as well as plump cushions for napping.

Gracious to guests, she was always generous to those who felt thirst and hunger or who sought work on her vast lands.

*   *   *

Yet some creatures grumbled about Siti's wealth and her family. The nightly songfests of the kits, who, despite their tutoring, yowled off-key, disgruntled one crocodile.

"Enough!" he bellowed, driven mad by their din.

Raising his knobby snout, the crocodile gnashed his yellow teeth, snapped his powerful jaws, and bawled, "Not one more night will I let discordant yowls disturb my sleep! Siti's kits have damaged my ears long enough!"

As clouds shrouded the moon's rays, he assembled all Siti's neighbors. Only a mouse to whom she had given an herbal remedy for a sore tooth refused to attend the secret meeting. All those in attendance muttered their discontent. Furtively, they plotted.

A few days later, Siti left her estate, bound for Alexandria on a litter hoisted by four jackals. She hoped to barter a silo of her grain for a new tapestry woven by a renowned spider of that great city. She left the kits in their nanny's care.

The assassins knew the journey would require her stay in Alexandria for at least two days.

That night, after they'd ceased their lessons in yowling, the kits' nanny settled each of them on a bed piled high with silken cushions.

As the waxing sickle moon harvested the sky, the malcontents crept into Siti's home. Brandishing flaming torches, they set ablaze the boxwood and ebony furniture, the priceless painting of a feline hunt, and an intricately woven carpet from Persia.

Flames scorched the walls and fingered the doors in the rooms where the kits slept. Waking, they wailed piteously for help, but no one rescued them, for the rebels had also locked the doors to the servants' quarters, which they also burned to the ground.

All perished in the inferno.

Chuckling, the crocodile who'd led the rebellion bellowed, "Let the whole place burn down! Let Siti return to nothing but ashes."

He raised his snout high and thundered, "Siti's mother, her grandmother, and her great-grandmother knew only vast fortune. They never toiled or tilled the land. They never dirtied their paws with the labor that bends our backs and destroys our youth!"

Howls of agreement echoed up and down the valley as the arsonists leaned against the brick wall so as to savor the blaze. Their din mingled with the crackle of fire, waking all who slept in the village.

The crocodile snapped his teeth in delight. "Let Siti sift the ashes. She'll not find one treasure that's eluded our flaming torches."

Smoke billowed around all of them gathered by Siti's crumbling villa. Hungry tongues of fire lit the shadows of the night.

Tinged with the orange of sizzling flames, the crocodile laughed raucously and shouted, "When she has nothing, Siti will come to us for food. We'll be the generous ones. She'll toil and beg and live each day desperate for sleep with her belly growling for food and her mind longing for dreams!"

"So be it!" the arsonists shouted.

"Soil her pool! Cut down her palm trees!" the crocodile commanded.

"Break into her storerooms! Carry away all food and drink, clothing and sandals, jars of oil and clotted cream, wagons and litters," he ordered.

"Burn down her silos! Pull out the vines in her vineyards! Cut down her date palms!" he bellowed.

"Trample her bulrushes! Flatten her brick kilns! Auger holes into the bows of her feluccas and rip their lateen sails!" he shrieked as smoke encompassed him so that the other malcontents heard only his booming voice.

"So be it!"

"Desecrate her shrines so that not one brick rests on another! Salt her fields so that no furrow will yield harvest!" he coughed.

"Take everything from her. Then she'll be needy. Then she'll yowl, but no one will give her what none of us has ever had—security!"

Each disgruntled rebel hurried away to accomplish his wicked intentions. Soon all that was left of the vast estate was soot and ash.

Elated by their deeds, the arsonists returned to their homes where they recounted their treachery to their families. Many praised them.

Others did not. Remembering the many times Siti had been a kind and good neighbor, they insisted she was unlike many felines who arrogantly felt themselves superior to all other creatures.

The arsonists dismissed the memory of any kind deeds Siti had done. For them, she was only a reminder of their misery.

Chapter 5
Lady Siti Patiently Waits

When Siti returned home two days later, she found only desolation. Charred bones lay scattered where the nursery had stood. With each gust of wind, the ash of servants and slaves billowed across the deserted courtyard.

The creatures who had destroyed Siti's life stood in silence, eager for her to curse Bastet-Net who'd created them subservient. Siti had known both fortune and fame. Now, she would know bitterness and destitution.

As her neighbors hovered near the ash and rubble, Siti approached them. "My friends," she purred, "you've often come to me, weary from your labors, heavy with debt, overcome by grief, and I have had the means to comfort you—food from my table, coins from my money belt, and concern for your need."

Siti paused to survey the scene before her. Her neighbors looked everywhere but at her. They, too, surveyed the ashes and the soot. They smelt the odor of their deeds. Many began to twitch their tails and shake their heads. Some covered their eyes and moaned of disaster.

Then, once again, Siti began to miaow. "I have no jobs to give you now. No longer do I have food or money, for fortune has deserted me. Yet as long as Bastet-Net dreams her dream of me, I'll welcome you to share your own grief with me."

Hearing this, Siti's neighbors—even the crocodile who'd led the revolt—wept for their cowardly deeds. Throughout that day, Siti and her neighbors praised Bastet-Net for the wonder of their breath and the beat of their hearts.

"The great god of cats will provide," Siti assured them. "She'll care for all of us."

One by one, the creatures who'd tried to destroy the life of Siti marked their faces with ash and wailed repentance.

As the sun set over the river of the great valley, the crocodile invited Siti to rest in his home. "Here," he yipped, "you can decide what next to do."

How sweetly Siti thanked her benefactor as she followed him to his mud-brick dwelling by the marshes bordering the Nile. All through the night, Siti prayed one refrain:

> *Mine is the dream*
> *of the great god of cats.*
> *O, Bastet-Net, I praise You.*

During that time of grief, a great tremor shook the earth of the gold and copper mines Siti owned in Nubia and the Sinai. The deep caverns collapsed; only the overseers were left alive. No gold or copper would be mined until Siti gave them funds to hire new workers to build shafts.

Having nothing, she thanked the overseers for their service and bid them return to their homes in Syria. And still she chanted,

> *Mine is the dream*
> > *of the great god of cats.*
> *O, Bastet-Net, I praise you.*

*   *   *

On the seventh night after she'd lost all, Siti dreamed of Bastet-Net and heard her purr.

> *My little one,*
> > *you please me mightily.*
> *Many years ago I gave nine commands to Mosi,*
> > *the first feline who enchanted me.*
> *Let us remember these commands together.*

In her dream, Siti and the great god of cats yowled, one by one, the nine commands. For each of the first seven, Bastet-Net purred, "This you have done well."

When they dreamed the eighth command—"Hunt ruthlessly, but always with stealth."—Bastet-Net reproved Siti.

> *My dear one,*
>> *you do not follow this command.*
>
> *Servants hunt for you.*
>
> *You must reclaim the stalk,*
>> *the crouch, the pounce.*
>
> *I beseech you—*
>> *practice the hunt!*

"I shall," Siti promised.

Finally, in her dream, Siti and Bastet-Net yowled the ninth command given to all felines: "Remember that you are extraordinary because I, Bastet-Net, made you so." It was then that Bastet-Net truly admonished Siti.

> *Like so many felines,*
>> *you've forgotten why you are a remarkable*
>> *being.*
>
> *You've given credit only to yourself*
>> *for your graciousness and goodness,*
>> *your mercy and kindness.*

Puzzled, Siti inquired, "O Great God of Cats, to whom should I give credit if not to myself? Was it not my wealth that helped all?"

The great god of cats sighed her sweet breath upon Siti and then recounted her creation of sky, rain, sun, earth, and all creatures. Siti exclaimed, "Thank you, O Bastet-Net!" to each purr of creation.

Having relived creation, the great god of cats quizzed Siti. "Am I not generosity and goodness, graciousness and mercy?"

In her dream, Siti rolled over on her back so that her white belly faced the great god of cats. "Truly you are, O Bastet-Net. Because you are so good, you dream the dream in which you have enfolded me these many years."

With her sweet breath, Bastet-Net ruffled the fur on Siti's belly. Together they basked in their dream.

Then Siti miaowed her confusion. "What is the meaning of your deepest rumblings?" she asked. "I, too, am generous and good, gracious and merciful, and yet you fault me."

Bastet-Net smiled her sweetest smile and purred her deepest wisdom.

To be exceptional, my little one, is to know,
deep down in the pith of my sweet purr,
that my graciousness created you.

You are peerless only because I am.

For that you must purr gratitude.

Who would not be grateful for the wonder
of being encompassed by my dream?
You purr within my own deep-bellied purr.

"Then I am Thou?" Siti asked.

"You are."

Siti's dream ended, yet she continued to nap, secure in the presence of the great god of cats.

When she woke, she heard, in stillness, the purr of Bastet-Net. "My daughter, I will send good mews to all felines. A kit will be born in Egypt who will announce for me this good mews. All felines will rejoice. Hear then my yowl!"

This purr and what Siti had learned in that night's dream became the refrain that accompanied her for the remainder of her life.

* * *

The next night, Siti went out into the wilderness to learn again the hunt and stalk. In the following weeks, she bartered her work for those of her neighbors. She offered fine hairballs to bundle into mats for sleeping. The sale of these helped her build a hut amidst the soot and ashes of her old home.

Days passed into months and thence to years. Siti grew old, but she never forgot her dream nor the liquid love in the almond eyes of the great god of cats. Each night she prayed aloud.

> *O Great God of Cats,*
> *all that I am is Thou.*

> *If I am gracious,*
> *it is because*
> *You clothe me in your graciousness.*

If I am merciful,
  it is because
  You dream me in kindness.
If I am generous,
  it is because
  You are all-giving.
If I am good,
  it is because
  You enfold me in Your own goodness.
I am Thou, O Bastet-Net!
I await Your promise of a kit
  who will bring us good mews.
Do not forsake us, O Bastet-Net,
  for all we are is Thou.

The night came when Sirius, the brightest star in the heavens, rose on the eastern horizon. It was then that Siti welcomed the boundless breath of Bastet-Net. Together, they dream.

Chapter 6
Bastet-Net Yowls through Kosey

Bastet-Net wearied of felines who'd forgotten the nine commands she'd given first cat. They no longer remembered the gratitude Mosi had purred; they refused to curve themselves into the dream of the great god of cats.

Countless felines neglected her. They forgot that creatures served them because Bastet-Net had bestowed comeliness on cats.

Bemused by themselves, they grew fat and lazy. No longer did they unsheathe their claws to seek prey. They refused to exert themselves except to twitch their whiskers in command.

Dreaming her displeasure, Bastet-Net took action. She yowled a prophecy to Kosey.

The great god of cats chose Kosey as her prophet even though he was not the one who would announce the good mews. Another kit, at a future time, would fulfill the prophecy Bastet-Net had purred to Siti.

Kosey, the runt of his litter, had been born on the Isle of Philae, as it floated on the great river. When he was old enough to appreciate wisdom, his mother helped him discover his deepest heartwish—to serve the great god of cats.

Under his mother's tutelage, Kosey became known on the island as one who followed the ways of Bastet-Net. He treasured her nine commands and scratched them on the walls of his room.

As he settled into sleep each night, he thanked the great god of cats for her gracious commands.

For eight years, Kosey tilled the soil of his mother's land, scattering seed and harvesting. Surprisingly, one day in his ninth year, he heard a sweet purring sway the palm branches as he furrowed a field. A sudden wind warmed his flanks. The overpowering scent of Bastet-Net's holiness filled his nostrils.

Kosey fell to the ground and rolled over onto his back to turn his belly to the gaze of the great god of cats. Bastet-Net then yowled her command.

Leave this field.

Go out into all of Egypt.

Pad beyond the valley
  to the desert and the wilds of Sinai.

Journey from the delta
to where the Nile rises far to the south.

Announce to all felines that I grow weary
of the pride they take in themselves.

It is I who purr their beauty!

I who round their bellies
into the memory of my dream!

Without me, they are as reed pipes
that know no breath.

Announce, too, that good mews is coming!

A kit will be born who will proclaim this mews!

Take hope!

Live in expectation!

"I will do as you command, O Bastet-Net!" Kosey yowled.

The great god of cats continued to prophesy through him.

Warn all felines
that while all creatures serve my sweet purr,
they will rebel if cats forget
that I am grace and mercy,
goodness and generosity.

Only because of my purr are you unique.

One is coming who will know in the deep center of
herself
    that I am goodness and generosity.

She it is who will give you good mews
    that will content you.

My favored one,
    deliver my message
    to all of Egypt and beyond!

Know that I purr within you.

With this assurance, Bastet-Net's voice grew silent within Kosey. Palm branches ceased to sway; clouds drifted away. All was quiet in the furrowed field.

*   *   *

In the space of a yawn, Kosey left his plough and spent long years within the command of Bastet-Net.

"Beware, felines," he admonished each clowder of cats he encountered. "Change your ways. Twitch your ears joyfully. Pray your gratitude for the gifts of the great god of cats."

Gazing cross-eyed at the cats, Kosey yowled, "The great god of cats created you from the purr of her deep chest. You are Bastet-Net's creatures. You are phenomenal to all others, but not to the great god of cats."

No matter how large or small the clowder, all the cats refused to listen. Again and again, Kosey exhorted them. "If you resist this call," he warned, "your fur will fall out in lumps. Prey will turn on you. Sleep will elude you. Litters will rise up and snap your rumps!"

The cats only hissed disbelief.

Still, Kosey continued to announce Bastet-Net's warnings. "Mouse and vole shall rise up against you. Fish shall elude you. Fowl shall cackle at your hunger," he miaowed.

"All grace will leave you so that squirrel shall laugh at your ungainly stretch, your oafish yawn, your clumsy leap," Kosey wailed.

Hearing this, cats sauntered away, yawning.

Kosey journeyed to Syria, belaboring all cats with Bastet-Net's message: "You ungrateful felines! How often have you forgotten the great good god who created all beings and filled them with wonderment before your cunning?"

Miaowing softly, he shared the prophecy he'd received: "Bastet-Net promises that a kit will bring us good mews. Prepare yourself to hear her yowl lest mites deprive you of hearing."

Only derision met his prediction of doom.

Twice felines chased Kosey from their villages, snapping at his tail. Five times, they tossed him into dank prisons with no windows. They refused him milk and herring.

Once they thrust him into a deserted mine where he tumbled down the shaft into darkness. There he lay for seven days until a kind canine took pity on him and brought him back into the warmth of day.

The hound, glancing furtively from left to right, advised the bedraggled prophet to leave the village. "The other cats plan to cut off your tail, snip your whiskers, pull out your claws!" he woofed.

Grateful for the canine's help, Kosey sailed down river to another village, but there, too, he met only belligerence. Everywhere, cats tried to silence him.

They turned from him in distaste in every village and town. Ignoring the yowl of Bastet-Net, they lived in sumptuous pleasure, remaining blind to the hatred servitude had wrought in others.

When Kosey brought his failure to Bastet-Net, she consoled him.

You do well, my favored one!

You do all I ask of you!

Take comfort in my sweet purr.

Soon I will curve my body around you
and enfold you in my dream.

At the command of Bastet-Net, Kosey finally padded home to the Isle of Philae. Within the moon's cycle, the great god of cats gathered him into her dream. She pierced his marrow with the all-knowing light of her almond eyes. He now dreams forever within her purr.

Chapter 7
Runihura Plots Feline Destruction

A few years later, a canine called Runihura began to serve a wealthy feline mistress in Gizeh. In the distant past, this cat's ancestors had prowled the delta to protect inhabitants from witches that tormented night.

For this protection, the creatures of Lower Egypt willingly bowed before the phenomenal talent of this family of felines who hunted so diligently. In awe, the creatures served these cats for countless years.

However, Runihura's mistress, the descendant of those early feline hunters, had long since lost her ability to prowl stealthily. In her lethargy, she'd grown portly.

For two years, Runihura, a shrew canine served this tubby cat. Then, disgusted with her yellowing teeth, he refused to labor any longer for her.

"What right does she have to command me?" he complained to the other slaves of his mistress. "I am of noble descent. My father was of the Basenji family, natives of Nubia."

He glanced around the kitchen, aware that the other creatures there—especially the dogs—held him in some esteem. Encouraged, he continued to share the story of his ancestry. "My father served as a hunter for the felines in

Nubia, who'd grown lazy and refused to snare their own food."

Hearing this, the other creatures bleated and woofed their own stories of felines who had grown fat, lazy, and stingy. Runihura continued his tale. "My father had a way of chortling his remarks. A cat, newly arrived from Abyssinia, took exception to this."

The cook, a brindled canine also from Nubia, yapped her dismay that anyone would be ill-disposed to a chortle. Runihura thanked her for understanding and continued his saga.

"This accursed cat—who had the gall not to like the way my father woofed—paid a mob of scruffy felines— common cats who lived in alleys—to chase him beyond the city walls. But like all felines, they had no staying power and stopped along the road to groom themselves and snooze!"

All the listeners nodded for they knew the laziness of cats. Runihura now came to the climax of his story. "Father trotted north, following the Nile toward the Great Sea. Soon he sauntered into Gizeh. It was here he met and married my mother. She, too, was of noble descent, a daughter of the house of Saluki."

Runihura concluded his story with a booming bark. "Our family has served felines well for many lowly years. But no longer!"

*   *   *

When Runihura's feline mistress heard that he'd complained of bondage, she summoned him to her boudoir. There, arrayed in marmalade, she reclined on a silken cushion.

Subservient mice, awaiting her bidding, surrounded their rotund mistress. To her chagrin, Runihura did not bow before her. Instead, he looked directly into her eyes.

"You wastrel!" she yowled. "Who are you to defy me?"

Runihura merely grumbled deep in his throat.

"Lower your eyes!" his mistress ordered. "Remember all that is owing to your betters."

Hearing this command, Runihura growled—a deep, rumbling growl the like of which his mistress had never heard before.

Outraged, she flattened her ears. Arching her back, the portly feline tumbled from her silken cushions and slashed her claws across Runihura's nose.

Runihura, forgetting the obedience owed a mistress, snapped her neck and defiantly tossed her limp body into a far corner of the room. Standing tall on his muscular legs, Runihura bayed his triumph.

The attendant mice scurried under the chaise longue squeaking astonishment. Because they had never heard the story of Siti's kits, they thought this was the first time a dog had killed a cat. Jumping up and down on their teensy feet, they clapped their delight and praised Runihura's bravery.

Now the blood lust rose in Runihura. Racing to the marketplace, he urged all canines in Gizeh to overthrow feline domination. "No longer are we chattel!" he barked. "Come, you shepherds, warriors, and gladiators. Follow me!"

All the dogs in Gizeh crowded round Runihura as he outlined his plan. "We'll fight these felines! Never again will we entertain them with our death. We'll never shepherd their herds of skittering mice. Rise up! Together, we'll overthrow the tyranny of felines!"

Throughout Gizeh, canines harkened to Runihura's command. Warriors and gladiators stormed the palatial homes of felines and snapped the stout necks of all who lived within.

Afterward, they hired crocodiles to drag the feline bodies to the river and dump them into the flowing water. Nightly the crocodiles who dwelt along the river ate the bloated bodies that bobbled in the Nile.

Before deposing of the bodies, however, the frenzied canines nipped off the tails of all the corpses and carried them as trophies to the city square. There they affixed the limp appendages to hemp ropes and strung them across the marketplace.

For days that spanned weeks, those lifeless tails dangled in the breeze until the stench of rotting flesh assailed the delicate noses of the rebellious canines. Then they hired rats as street cleaners to rid the marketplace of the offending offal.

*   *   *

Soon Runihura's revolution spread up and down the valley of the great river. Few felines were safe from the wrath that canines had harbored for long years of subjugation.

The canines, sprinting from village and town, city and metropolis, toppled felines from their heedless rule, executing those they most despised.

Canines rounded up any felines who tried to flee the city. Sniping at tails and paws, they drove them back to the marketplace where they sold many cats to the highest bidder among the creatures gathered there—crocodile, ibis, canine, jackal, oxen, donkey.

Soon the coup spread beyond the confines of Egypt.

Led by Runihura, a contingent of canine troops tramped north to Syria where a mighty band of Saluki joined them. Within days, they crossed the Tigris and Euphrates and loped east to Tibet. There, the ancient family of Mastiffs enlisted in the mutiny.

Another legion of mercenaries sailed the Great Sea to Macedonia and Italy. All other creatures who despised feline caprice and conceit joined the fray. They bayed, snarled, oinked, grunted, and bleated their abhorrence.

Countless rebels squealed, chirruped, and brayed.

Many bellowed, chirred, droned, quacked, and hooted.

Others cawed, squawked, trumpeted, and screeched.

Multitudes hissed, whinnied, lowed, nickered, and gobbled.

Thus, in a cacophony of disdain, they renounced servitude and cast cats out of house and home. The rebels hounded them into the wilderness, then built walls to keep all cats from returning and hired jackals to keep the studded gates locked.

Furtively, cats slunk into forest and field, but everywhere—in every thicket, on every mountain, in every river valley, on every prairie and steppe, in every desert—insurgents lurked.

These mutinous renegades trapped, tortured, and executed any feline not wily enough to elude them. Sometimes they simply throttled befuddled felines, but often they crucified, flayed alive, roasted, or threw them from mountain crags.

The canines gleefully tarred and feathered many a haughty feline. Geese willingly let themselves be plucked so as to participate in this humiliation. The geese then donned tunics woven by silk worms freed from feline mistresses.

The malevolent mongrels dug traps and covered them with branches on which they strewed sweet-smelling herbs. Thus did they ensnare unwary felines. The canine scoundrels sunk so low as to use the felines' favorite minty aphrodisiac, which was named after them.

As these ruses ensnared the cats, they balefully mewled bewilderment. Why were creatures who had once served them so willingly now rebelling?

Chapter 8
Mafuane Sails to Britain

The prophet Kosey had died, and the canine insurrection was raging when Bastet-Net called another cat—the lowborn Mafuane. The great god of cats yowled that cats and canines were doomed unless all accepted her good mews of deliverance.

Mafuane had been born in the delta seven years before Runihura killed his mistress and called all canincs to rebel. Mafuane was not a pureblood Mau like those ancient felines who first ruled Egypt. Instead, she was descended from cats who disdained command. They had migrated to the marshes long before her birth.

However, from the beginning, the indolent felines of the nearby towns scolded these common cats. "You denizens of the delta refuse to accept our right to respect!"

A few haughty felines paw-printed their scorn on papyrus scrolls and nailed them to stalls in the marketplace.

"You marsh cats betray us!" the posters proclaimed. "Your yowls remain uneducated; your paw prints illiterate. You shame all felines with the life you live. What are other creatures to think when they sniff such as you?"

Mafuane and her littermates learned from their mother that many felines reclined on silken cushions, too lazy to sniff the scents surrounding them. These self-important felines refused to greet moon and stars with yowls of praise for Bastet-Net. Instead they snoozed throughout both night and day, always served by other creatures.

Often Mafuane's mother described the obstinacy of those felines who refused to follow the commands of the great god of cats.

"The truest command of Bastet-Net is to nurture the kits she bestows on us," her mother miaowed. "But many felines no longer honor this command. Slaves and servants raise the young of these haughty cats."

Mafuane and her littermates listened attentively when their mother purred, "No longer are these felines sleek and lean! They're plump with laziness, unwilling to follow Bastet-Net's command to hunt."

As Mafuane and her littermates pressed against their mother's warm belly, she yowled examples of how many felines ignored the great god of cats and her commands. "Felines in fine palaces have forgotten how to pounce on prey. How to stalk. How to crouch and leap."

Stopping for a few moments, to groom her litter, the mother then purred, "Only in Bastet-Net's final command do they excel—they purr pleasure at their own peerlessness! But they've turned the awe of other creatures into servitude."

*   *   *

Mafuane's mother nurtured her and the young kit grew lean and lithe. When fully grown, she and her littermates journeyed south to Memphis, a city upriver from the delta. There she worked for a full-blooded Mau, sewing lengths of linen into parasols to ward off the sun's bright rays.

Her brothers labored on the docks where they unloaded boats, mended torn lateen sails, and toted goods into the marketplace. Like Mafuane, they watched as malevolence simmered within the breath of all creatures who served the ruling felines. In Mafuane's seventh year, that seething animosity boiled over.

It was then that the canine Runihura rebelled in Gizeh. As his tyranny spread, many felines who worked for merchants in Memphis or on the docks slunk into hiding. Mafuane and her brothers found a snug cave in the hills beyond the great river.

When the new moon rose, they left their cave and crept down to the delta. Stealthily they entered their old home. There they found their mother asleep. Gently they nudged her to wakefulness, beseeching her to go with them into hiding.

She nudged each of their noses with hers, but refused to leave her home. "I await the dream of the great god of cats. Her ways are mysterious," she purred. "The moon rises and the sun sets in her eyes as in ours. This rebellion is but the rising of the sun and its setting. More starry nights lie beyond."

With their mother's purr echoing within them, Mafuane and her brothers left the delta and stole back to their cave. A month later, a poor feline fleeing Memphis sought refuge with them in their cave.

That night, he described how the insurgency had spread to the delta. A pack of crazed canines had stomped the shores of the great river and the surrounding marshes to capture any felines who crouched there. They had seized Mafuane's mother and roasted her—along with a score of other wailing cats.

Hearing this, Mafuane and her brothers resolved to leave Egypt. When her brothers purred Mafuane goodbye and padded westward to the desert, she stole aboard a boat and sailed to Britain. There she lived in a forest outside London.

As terrified felines fled the city, news of sedition came to Mafuane each night. Often these fugitives stayed for a day or two in the small hut she'd built in the branches of a chestnut tree.

*   *   *

In Mafuane's second year of exile, Bastet-Net called her to prophesy. The Egyptian feline was napping when the sharp-toothed leaves shadowing her hut trembled. As the tail of Bastet-Net wafted the air, a canticle of praise radiated within Mafuane.

Then all was silent, except for the thrum of her heart. In the midst of that silence, Bastet-Net touched Mafuane's nose with hers.

Rise, my daughter.

Climb to the highest branch
  of this chestnut tree
  and proclaim the message
  I will give you!

Yowl it by night and day
  to felines and canines alike!

Mafuane began to tremble. "How can I, O Great God of Cats? The rebels will kill me!"

Hearing her plea, Bastet-Net purred.

Be still, Mafuane!

Be still and listen!

I made all creatures.

Because of me, they can
  howl or bark,
  nicker or gobble,
  bellow or bleat!

In their defiance,
  they've forgotten my goodness
  and graciousness,
  my mercy and faithfulness.

They now take pride only in themselves.

You must remind them of this.

Tell them, too, that I will yowl good mews
when the time is right
and a kit of great sweetness is born in Egypt.

"But they'll kill me!" Mafuane wailed.
Seeing Mafuane's fear, Bastet-Net comforted her.

Do not fear.
My sweet breath will protect you.
My tail will swipe away any who try to capture
you.
My claws will score the bodies of those who seek
your death.
Be not afraid, Mafuane, my little prophetess.
I, Bastet-Net, am with you!

*   *   *

The next day, Mafuane, the lowly feline from the delta marshes of Egypt, began to proclaim her message. She admonished felines, reminding them of their dissolute lives.

"You have renounced Bastet-Net's ways and forgotten her commands," Mafuane yowled. "Remember that your superiority comes from her, not from yourselves! When you have learned this, harmony will once again infuse your life."

Pausing to sniff a passing breeze, Mafuane continued, "But until that time you will know only strife and terror, death and destruction! You must change your ways. If you do not, you will not hear the good mews that Bastet-Net intends to yowl."

Hearing this, the canines in the crowd began to bark their scorn. Mafuane yowled, "Beware all you who relish the servitude of felines. Soon, Bastet-Net will wake from slumber and pounce on you and your mangy cohorts."

The canines simply laughed raucously and sniggered at her scruffy coat of fur. Mafuane ignored their taunts and yowled even louder, "What does the great god of cats ask of you? That you live in peace with all creatures—even cats!"

Soon all creatures in Britain had heard Mafuane's cry. Felines who'd fled there from far-away Egypt confided that Bastet-Net's message had even reached the Nile valley. The great god of cats, true to her word, protected Mafuane.

In London, the captain of the canine guards called Mafuane a claw in his side. He and his troops grew weary of hunting her, for Bastet-Net protected her wanderings, cloaking Mafuane with darkness and shadow.

Yet most felines, insisting that the rebels would soon come to heel, turned their backs on Mafuane. Still, for five years, she stole up and down Britain. Then the great god of cats called her to dwell forever within her dream. There Mafuane purrs her message still.

Chapter 9
Osaze Fights for Freedom

As Mafuane toiled in Britain, the canine rebellion spread over the known world. However, the mongrels had underestimated felines. It was true many cats had grown both fat and lazy. In fact, because of the indolence of most felines, the rebels had never before experienced their inborn wiliness.

That was about to change. Their flight from the ravaging canines had compelled felines to exercise once again the agility, the adroitness, the deftness that Bastet-Net had bestowed on them as their birthright.

Soon, many feline fugitives grew sleek and lean, able to wield their ancient gifts of stealth, pounce, and stalk. A few—but only a paltry few—vowed to sharpen their claws, unsheathe them, and thwart their enemy.

One of these few, Osaze the Zealot, became the most renowned resistance fighter of his time even though he had only one eye—he'd lost his other in a brawl on the docks.

Despite this, Osaze took to the mountains east of Syria and dwelt in caves. From crags, he tossed stones onto unwary canine scouts below, leaping nimbly to the road to slash their flanks. He left these mongrels whining regret for having rebelled against feline domination.

Osaze encouraged other Syrian cats to band with him, but they refused to follow this tawny feline whom they found too enthusiastic for their taste. These recalcitrant laggards believed only in their own uniqueness and their ability to cajole.

"We need no one but ourselves!" they insisted. "Surely, this motley mob that torments us will soon realize that without us they are nothing! Each of them needs at least one feline to content their lives! Soon they'll miss the harmony of our purr!"

"You foolish felines!" Osaze yowled. "Canines, jackals, wolves, crocodiles, oxen pursue you to the death; yet you refuse to resist! These craven scamps have lost their taste for slavery. Follow me or lose all!"

His message failed to win over these pleasure-loving cats. They wanted only the rich cream they'd supped in their palatial homes. None could see the advantage of being led by such a common cat.

After all, Osaze hadn't lived a sumptuous life. Instead, he'd worked in the bazaar, selling paw-printed linen scarves to tourists.

"You moonstruck idiots!" Osaze muttered, disappearing into a cleft in the mountainside.

From there, he waged an unremitting battle against those who had challenged the superiority of cats. It was true he'd never used his perfection to distinguish himself. However, Osaze, like all felines, had always accepted the mediocrity of other creatures.

"No canine has the right to defy us," Osaze asserted, "whether we felines choose to wield our superiority or not!"

* * *

Soon Osaze's exploits reached distant Tibet. There, Runihura, the leader of the canine mutiny, accompanied his troops in their march across Asia.

Among his soldiers was an Afghan hound who'd served him faithfully since they'd met on the foothills of Hindu Kush. The supreme alpha, with lip curled, ears erect, and tail rigid, barked an angry message to this obedient hound.

The dutiful courier raced westward, fleet as wind, to Damascus. There he delivered Runihura's message to the renowned Saluki warrior who governed Syria for the alpha.

With head cocked, the governor listened intently as the Afghan hound woofed Runihura's command: "Track down this feline named Osaze and eliminate him! If we permit his harassment of our troops, other felines will doubt our power. Ask no questions! Simply kill any cat who dares resist us!"

Within days, the canine governor devised a plan to capture Osaze. According to his spies, the resistance fighter hid in a cave within the mountains. The governor planned to first lead his troops in the deep stillness of night to the mountain range.

At that point, he'd command his aide—an intelligence falcon—to fly high over every cliff and canyon until she sighted Osaze. This trusted bird of prey would then signal the governor and his soldiers with a two-pitched keen. Hearing this, they would rush forward and attack.

That very night, the governor executed the first part of his plan. His Saluki warriors trotted over sand dunes to the foot of the mountains. As a sickle moon rose, the contingent rested, plotting how they would seize Osaze, mutilate his sinewy body, and send his spirit slinking into the dismal dream of Bastet-Net.

They had just reached their destination when three hounds, tempted by a hare, deserted. Ever sharp-eyed, the governor snarled, "Stop, you fools! All creatures, even hares, have banded together to rid themselves of felines! Forget your old enmities! I order you to return to your post!"

(In his anger, the governor had conveniently forgotten that most canines still found roasted hare tasty.)

Two of the warriors slunk back, but the third, seeing the hare race into the underbrush, bounded away. As he disappeared over the horizon, the other soldiers loudly rebuked his treachery. Their mighty din filled the plateau and rose into the mountains. Thus it was that a frivolous hare and a foolish Saluki saved Osaze's life.

Osaze waited until the contingent of canine warriors below him fell asleep. When darkness cloaked both desert and mountain, he sidled from the cavern and crept down the western side of the range toward the Great Sea.

He padded to a Syrian port where he bribed a canine sailor to sneak him on board a ship bound for Carthage.

*   *   *

A few days later, Osaze stepped onto dry land. He immediately journeyed into the vast desert far south of Carthage. There he found many cats living a life of drudgery and wariness.

Determinedly, Osaze attempted to rally these scruffy felines into resistance but, once again, met with little success. However, he did convince a few to accept tutelage in the ancient art of slash and claw, bite and rip.

As days passed, the reluctant recruits grudgingly learned to stretch their legs and arch their backs in an attack. They practiced the art of bristling. Each day, they exercised the muscles of their ears so as to show the backs of them in battle.

Day in and day out, Osaze instructed the Tunisian felines in the fine art of the intimidating yowl. He taught them to advance against an enemy slowly, stealthily. Long into night, they practiced the scornful glare and the raised head, tilted to one side.

But the willful cats, despite their training, still refused to follow Osaze into battle against the marauding canines.

"We're solitary creatures," they insisted. "We follow no one!"

A cat from Alexandria complained, "You're like those who hound us! Like them, you seek to change us. No one, not even Bastet-Net, can fashion us into slaves!"

"Soon those rascals will realize that without us they are nothing," added a feline from Phoenicia. "We're a boon to all other creatures!"

"Yes!" shouted all the recruits, who, despite their training, still insisted on spending most days napping, longing for the past. "Who can deny that we are exquisite beings?"

Osaze listened to these feckless mewls with growing impatience. Finally, he leaped upon the ridgepole of a tent to reprove the recalcitrant cats lounging on the desert sands.

"You're as foolish as the felines of Syria!" he hissed. "Only if we act together can we hope to gain the respect due us! You're too lazy to resist. I denounce you!"

Osaze licked his right paw one last time, brushed it over his right ear, twitched it, leaped down from the ridgepole, and moseyed away, yowling a song of petition to the great god of cats.

Crush our enemies, O Bastet-Net!

Terrify those who seek our deaths!

Slay those who rejoice at our demise!

Gnash Your teeth;
   twitch Your whiskers;
   flatten Your ears!

Harrow them who rise up against us!

Howl mange on canines!
Decay the yellow teeth of crocodiles!
Molt ibises!
Straighten the coils of snakes!
Cripple jackals!
Weigh down the bulk of hippopotami!
Exterminate beetle and flea,
cockroach and fly!

Denounce the devious plans of those accursed
canines
who snap our necks, bite our rumps, nip our tails!
Quench the taste they have for rule!

It is You, O Great God of Cats,
who made felines exceptional.
You dreamed the awe
all creatures once offered us.
You purred our elegance and grace.
Then grind into dust
the canine desire to dominate!

This we ask, O Bastet-Net!
Destroy our enemies!
So that we may once again praise You!

Osaze now trekked northward across the desert and came again to Carthage. Weary, he snoozed a few days, but as the seventh night merged into day, he resolved once again to search out other cats who might choose to fight the canine coup.

Chapter 10
A Canine Seeks Détente

Osaze found respite from his fight against canine tyranny not from a cat, but from a dog. One night he lay napping in the upper room of a dilapidated inn in Carthage and failed to hear a canine approach. A gray Sloughi had come within five feet of Osaze before the tired freedom fighter sniffed his presence and woke, hissing disparagement.

"So!" Osaze shouted. "You accursed canines have finally foiled me! Put me to death, but other felines will rise up and resist you!"

(Of course, given his experience in the Tunisian desert, Osaze didn't believe this, but to yowl nothing to a canine was tantamount to betraying his race.)

"Shhh!" the Sloughi muttered. "I've come to help you."

Osaze instantly leaped onto the windowsill, ready to take advantage of the canine's failure to snap his neck.

"Wait!" the hound ordered. "Look at my right paw. There you'll see the mark of my own subjugation."

Curious, Osaze leapt to the floor and examined the mark on the hound's extended paw. Incised in its pad was the letter D. "That D stands for deserter," the hound explained.

Seeing this brand, Osaze settled on the rumpled bed. Throughout the long night, the Sloughi, whose name was

Jabari, complained that Runihura had become a tyrant. The alpha now ruled canines and other creatures with an iron paw.

Runihura was not content with simply overthrowing the control of felines. Now he wanted to shape the world into his empire.

Runihura persuaded canine underlings—from Morocco to the Sahara, into Egypt, up to Syria, across the land of the two rivers, beyond Tibet to China—to join him in his quest for domination.

Now his army hunted not only felines, but also gazelles, hares, jackals, and other creatures who didn't relish canine rule.

"I am descended from the family of Sloughi in Nubia!" Jabari rolled his eyes and twitched his gray muzzle as if the information should explain everything to Osaze. And so it did, for the family of Sloughi had long served the Abyssinian family of cats and the Egyptian Maus.

"For months after Runihura's mutiny began," Jabari continued, "we protected our feline rulers, but finally the alpha's troops overcame us and pressed us into accepting their wicked deeds."

The brave Sloughi explained to Osaze that many canines had grown weary of bloodshed. They desired peace because they longed to return home.

"I've tasted freedom and no longer want cats to command me," Jabari admitted. "But I don't want to rid the world of them!"

Next, Jabari woofed the names of other canine breeds who wanted only freedom. "Many Sloughi, Afghans, Basenjis, Salukis, Greyhounds, Tibetan Mastiffs, and other canine warriors have abandoned Runihura's army," he confided. "This accursed mark on my paw reveals all that has happened: I deserted, was captured and branded, and then fled again into the desert."

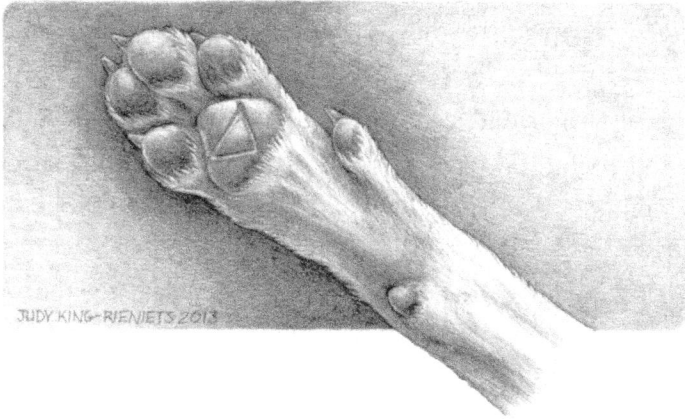

In the desert, Jabari, not sure what to do next, had trotted across the hot sand until he came to the encampment where Osaze had been conducting feline training. For long days, he'd watched the recruits study the art of resistance.

"Your felines will never be a match for a contingent of Runihura's army," Jabari warned. "However, I have a plan. If it's acceptable to you, canines would reign, but cats would live in peace among them."

At this woof, Osaze arched his back to reject the proposal. Seeing this, Jabari quickly added, "I have one piece of information that might sway your fierce pride into accepting this." Jabari then told Osaze about Publius, governor of the island of Malta.

"He won favor with Runihura by training a canine contingent in Persia," the Sloughi explained. "They fought against cats like yourself who resisted our rule."

Thus it was that from Jabari, a war-scarred dog, Osaze first learned of other feline freedom fighters like himself. They lived in the eastern realms and had fought the canine rebels for many moons.

According to Jabari, they fashioned bows and shot steel-tipped arrows at dogs who pursued them into the mountains.

Many cats chopped down trees to ambush travelers.

Others built rafts to ford the eastern rivers in the shadow of night so as to scale the walls of gated towns and harass the sleeping creatures within.

Hearing this, Osaze rejoiced that he was not the only feline with enough gumption to fight the enemy!

As sun dawned, Jabari explained that in Persia, Publius had gone into the prison where Runihura kept his captive cats. There, the warrior had come to appreciate the desire all creatures have for freedom. In the light of day, the Maltese still did what the alpha ordered, but secretly, he consoled the perplexed felines.

Runihura, unaware of this perfidy and in recognition of Publius' service in Persia, promoted him to governor of the island of Malta.

"He's an intelligent leader and a great yapper. If you were to approach him," Jabari advised, "he might have the wits to devise a plan that would stop this useless bloodshed."

Kneading his bed's comforter into a pleasing mound, Osaze settled himself and miaowed, "I am listening Jabari. Say something that can convince me to stop my fighting."

Lying down on the floor, Jabari, too, settled himself. Conspiratorially, he began to woof his thoughts. "You cats would have your place in a new order that you and Publius might devise. Some of you would know wealth and power again; others would be poor, but such is the way of all creatures."

Truly, Osaze thought, this canine—unlike the felines he'd met in his perambulations—was a philosopher.

* * *

The next evening, Osaze crept aboard a freighter bound for Malta. The ship, facing no ill winds, quickly reached shore. Immediately upon landing, Osaze searched out a friend of Jabari's who set about securing an audience with the governor.

Within the week, Osaze and Publius met to discuss the reign of Runihura. Fortunately for the weary resistance fighter, the Maltese governor did indeed want peace, just as Jabari had predicted in Carthage.

Publius sailed to Syria a few days later. There he met with the alpha of all canines. Weeks passed as this fearless Maltese rumbled and growled, grumbled and yelped, whined and yapped the plan that he and Osaze had worked out: Runihura would declare an armistice. Canines would govern, but in peace.

No longer would they hunt down unwary creatures—be they feline, hare, ibis, or gazelle. Instead, canines would exchange constant vigilance for détente. Feline resistance fighters would sheath their claws and cease to use cunning to entrap their enemies.

Runihura, weary himself of strife—and more than a little tired of the wiliness of felines—accepted Publius' proposition. His fleetest runners carried the news around his empire.

Soon the canine troops trotted home while most felines came out of hiding and returned to the great cities of Egypt and Syria, Tibet and China, Nubia, and the land surrounding the Great Sea.

Many local canine leaders welcomed them back into their provinces. In fact, Runihura hired a feline astrologer to predict the coming of earthquakes and tempests.

However, nearly all cats had to live in one-room huts. While many found these hovels beneath them, most were grateful for their lives.

As time passed, some cats prospered. They built fine homes again and hired jackals and canines, ibis and crocodiles to work for them. However, the felines still ate mice, fish, and birds because these skittish creatures hadn't organized themselves into unions.

Of course, Runihura was no one's fool. He remained vigilant. That is to say, he was aware that some felines still thought themselves better than all other creatures. Because of this, Runihura and his descendants never allowed cats to own slaves no matter how prosperous these felines became.

Yet one night in a dream, Bastet-Net visited Osaze and gave him a message: "A day will come when a comely cat will be born in Egypt with a new purr. She will free felines from having to serve the faults of others."

Osaze yowled this message from Bastet-Net whenever other felines came to visit him. After he entered the dream of the great god of cats, many sang his song in secret.

Praise! Praise and thanksgiving!

Praise to Bastet-Net who has sent tranquility
into the hearts of canines!

No longer do we felines bask in veneration,
but we triumph!
No longer do we rule,
but we grow strong in hope!

A feline will come to us.
All will know her sweetness.
All will bow before her wiles,
marvel at her yowl.

This is the dream of the Great God of Cats.
Praise Her! All praise to Bastet-Net!
Cateluia!

Chapter 11
Tabia Experiences a Dream

Within two years after Runihura accepted Publius' plan for détente, death came to the alpha. In the decades afterward, one canine after another ruled his empire.

In the eightieth year of the Canine Era, a new alpha appointed repressive underlings within the far-flung empire. To Egypt, he sent a governor—one Cirneco dell'Etna by name—who conducted a census. His minions recorded all creatures in Egypt—from beetles, fleas, and cats to lizards, snakes, and canines.

As Sirius rose on the eastern horizon, dell'Etna sent out three hundred minions to tally the creatures dwelling within the valley of the Nile. As a contingent arrived in Abydos, which lay across the river from Thebes, drought was squeezing dry the land of Egypt.

Lolling-Tongue Zuka, a sergeant in the squad, encountered a family of Maus inhabiting a one-room hut on the outskirts of Abydos. The mastiff counted three in the family: Sylvestris, the father; Felias, the mother; and Tabia, who was only a kit.

Zuka added three marks to his papyrus scroll, then demanded that Sylvestris state his occupation. The census-taker was sure of what the answer would be because canines had set a bounty on mice and rats. They considered such creatures criminals, worthy only of death.

Catching and deposing of such vermin was the job of the outcasts of canine society. Many cats relished this job for they got to eat what they captured. Others, however, complained that such work was beneath them.

Sylvestris, unimpressed with the canine's mien of authority, simply yawned and settled himself on the floor in an elegant curve. Outraged, Zuka shredded one of the father's ears.

Bristling, Tabia, the kit, attacked the mastiff's wide nose, drawing blood. Momentarily, he cowered before her. Then Zuka barred his teeth, remembering his standing in dell'Etna's battalion.

At that, Tabia began a sweet purring. Entranced, the dog fell into a deep sleep. When he woke, his nose bled no more, nor did any scar betray his wound. Moreover, the jagged edges of Sylvestris' right ear had been restored to their pristine perfection atop his rounded head.

"How did this happen?" Zuka asked, but Tabia, feeling no need to brag, simply sang another pleasing melody. Zuka left the house, convinced that he had met a feline who'd go far, even in the canine world.

Returning to Thebes, Zuka described his adventure to dell'Etna. "That kit is unique!" the census-taker woofed.

"Keep your eyes trained on this Tabia," dell'Etna ordered. "Watch her as she grows up. A kit such as this could lead all other cats against us."

* * *

When she grew out of kittenhood, Tabia became a renowned feline of frivolity. She left behind her parents and their hovel and moved into a local inn where she entertained every male cat who sought respite from canines.

Sylvestris and Felias moaned their distress, but Tabia only sang one of her soothing songs. They, too, like Zuka before them, fell under her trance.

For over a year, Tabia devoured fresh sardines, plump finches, tasty mice, and sliced vole. The strays she welcomed to her bed brought all these to her in payment for her sweet purr.

This talented cat, when not eating, yawing, or grooming her gleaming silver fur, entertained countless male felines whom others scorned as riff-raff.

During those months, Tabia did nothing to help the other felines of Abydos. Again and again, her parents beseeched their kit to use her charms to persuade others to rebel. Ignoring them, she continued to seek comfort and ecstasy.

Yet Bastet-Net will work her wile. Thus it was that in her fourth year, Tabia dreamed a powerful dream. In it, she miaowed a song that gathered all the felines of Abydos around her. In that mystic dream, Bastet-Net winningly purred a command.

Go out among the other cats of Egypt.

Give them this message:

Every feline has nine lives!

Rejoice!

The next day, Tabia woke early, padded to the marketplace, and settled comfortably upon the wall of the village well. There she began to expound her good mews of nine lives. Many creatures stopped to hear her melodious chirrup, but only felines stayed to listen for only cats were assured nine lives.

When the moon rose, Tabia returned to the inn to gather her belongings. She stuffed her cotton tunic with its blue edging, her sandals, and several jeweled collars into her knapsack. She left behind her linen quilts, her feather mattress, and her ornamented mirror.

Before leaving Abydos, she visited her parents and related her dream.

"We will miss you," Sylvestris miaowed, "but when Bastet-Net purrs, all felines must listen. She will protect you from enraged canines. Never will they accept that cats have more lives than they!"

"Bastet-Net did not neglect to purr that danger to me," Tabia miaowed. "But she assured me of her presence." She then rubbed noses, first with her mother, followed by her father. With this good-bye, she set out for the villages of the Delta.

Days later, Tabia met Sabah. This feline tax-collector, who labored for the canine government, eagerly shared with Tabia the story of her life in Heliopolis. First, she recounted the difficulties of working for teeth-snapping canines. Then she described the delight she took in exploring the canine tombs and temples of Heliopolis. They filled her with glee because the mongrels within them were dead.

"Cease to look among tombs and temples for signs of death," Tabia purred. "I have a message for you from Bastet-Net. She has given you the gift of nine lives. Follow me and announce this to all felines."

Hearing this, Sabah did not even return to her dwelling to collect her knapsack; she immediately followed Tabia.

Chapter 12
Bastet-Net Purrs within Tabia

For long months that stretched into a year, Tabia trekked up and down Egypt. Often she invited a cat who displayed a talent for yowling to join her in her journey. Together, she and her companions sailed upstream in their shallow boats. At other times, they meandered over dunes to proclaim the good mews of nine lives to felines hiding in the desert.

Hearing this good mews, felines from Alexandria, to Heliopolis, to Memphis, to Abydos, to Thebes rejoiced. Now they knew that only in this one life would they endure the misery of being subservient in the Canine Empire. In another life, they would surely have the satisfaction of dominion.

In Memphis, Tabia healed a feline—Masud—who worked in a tourist shop, creating hairball tapestries. Each time he failed to meet his daily quota, the owner of the shop, a cruel canine, bite off part of his employee's tail.

The day came when the despondent feline had nothing left but a mere nubbin that wagged pathetically as he approached Tabia. "No longer am I handsome!" Masud wailed. "Without my tail, I cannot leap gracefully!"

Tabia, whose own tail was sleek and curved to the warmth of Bastet-Net's breath, assured Masud that he'd know refinement once again. As the wind sheltered itself in silence, Tabia gazed fixedly into Masud's yellow eyes.

Slowly the woeful feline's tail grew until it reached a gratifying length. Ecstatically, Masud flicked it back and forth, curving its brown tip. Leaping into the air, he yowled a paean of praise:

> *Praise to Bastet-Net!*
>
> *Praise!*
>
> *I have a new tail!*
>
> *Rejoice with me!*

"I am glad you praise Bastet-Net," Tabia purred. "She gave you this fine tail. She blesses all felines with grace and beauty."

"Cateluia!" Tabia's companions shouted.

"Yes! Cateluia! In their pride, many of our ancestors forgot that their superlative graciousness is Bastet-Net's!" Tabia reminded them. "Because of that, other creatures turned against us and rebelled."

She looked around at her companions and purred sweetly. "Because we felines are uncommonly talented, all other creatures owe us respect, but they need not become slaves to awe. They, too, must serve only the great god of cats!"

"Cateluia!" Tabia's companions shouted again; Masud added his yowl to theirs. Together, they reclined beneath a date palm for a repast of roasted mouse and clotted cream.

As they were eating, Tabia turned to Masud. "Will you return to work for the Saluki?"

"I am poor, and I have no other work to do. So I must return."

"Don't you create superlative hairball tapestries?"

"So say the tourists."

"Then find other skillful felines to do the same."

In the years that followed, Masud kept Tabia's advice in mind. Thus it was that he became the owner of his own shop, which offered jobs to many felines who created tasteful hairballs carpets and wall hangings. Soon many creatures—even hounds—purchased their wares.

*   *   *

More days passed. Tabia and her companions sailed downstream to Alexandria. There they heard rumors that Bastet-Net's gift to felines had enraged the Egyptian governor.

Despite this, Tabia did not silence her message.

Instead, from beneath a billowing lateen sail, from the roofs of feline huts, and from the desert that bordered each Egyptian village and town, she yowled the good mews: Felines have nine lives!

It was in Alexandria that Tabia heard a great commotion along the dock. An unkempt feline, wearing a scruffy bronze coat with dark bands around it, barked before a group of gaping canines and jackals.

"Off! Off of me, you fleas and ticks!" the bedraggled feline woofed. "Off! Off of me! Bite me no longer!"

The tormented cat fell to the ground, rolled her green eyes, twitched her reddish brown tail, and barked ferociously, "Off! Off!"

JUDY KING-RIENIETS 2013

"What's wrong with her?" one of Tabia's companions asked.

"She's possessed. The spirits of mongrels have taken hold of her, so she yelps and barks as they do!"

Tabia padded forward to where the demon-riven feline lay panting in the dust. Touching her nose, Tabia ordered the demons to desist. "Out! Out! Out of her, you demon curs that mock this feline! 'Out!' I yowl!"

Nine canine spirits—in a cacophony of barking, yelping, growling, whining, moaning, woofing, whimpering, grumbling, and sighing—rose from the feline who now lay limp in the dust. Merging into mist, the demons gave one last mournful cry, then dissipated in the sun's rays.

"Stand up!" Tabia ordered the feline. "Stand up!"

The freed feline ceased to bark and rose as if in memory of a dream. She yawned widely, shook the dust from her tatty bronze coat, and began to groom herself, all the while purring contentment. Finally, feeling presentable once again, the feline introduced herself.

"I am Mavie. Who are you? And how did you send the demons away?"

"I am Tabia, beloved of the great god of cats, just as you, too, are beloved. You and I and Bastet-Net are One."

One of Tabia's companions offered the tattered feline a braised mole he had bought at a nearby stall and some sweet cow's milk. As she ate, Mavie recounted the mournful story of her life.

She had been born in Tenby, a port city in distant Wales. As a kit, she'd been able to purr as sweetly as a songbird. When she was old enough, her parents sent her into the market place. Each day, her songs captivated tourists.

One night a crew of canine sailors broke into her home, stole her away, and bound her to the mast of their ship. The ordered her to sing them home safely.

Throughout the journey from Wales to the Great Sea, the canine sailors

forced the frightened feline to purr her songs even as the swell of chilled waves splashed the deck, drenching her tabby coat. Reaching port, they tossed her onto a round-bottomed ship bound for Alexandria.

Sadly, Mavie could no longer sing because the sailors' treatment during the long journey had crazed her.

Hearing this, Tabia purred, "Bastet-Net desires your song. Return to Wales. Sing the good mews of nine lives. Your life has been hard. Only Bastet-Net knows what awaits you beyond today. So I purr to you the comfort of one message: Trust her."

Padding to a nearby inn, Tabia sniffed out shelter for Mavie. "When your strength returns," she advised the songstress, "sing here in Alexandria to raise money for your passage home to Wales."

Mavie thanked Tabia for all her help and settled into a long-awaited nap. Tabia placed a fleece-lined quilt over the bedraggled feline, then she and her companions continued on their way.

*　　*　　*

Hearing rumors of Tabia's travels, felines throughout Egypt yowled loud and long in the hope that she would come to proclaim the good mews to them. Because of this, the canine governor sent soldiers to quell the riots and impose a curfew. No longer could felines yowl until the sun rose.

Despite this curfew, Tabia and her companions found crowds of felines gathered silently along the shore when they reached Memphis. The cats there had posted a lookout on the nearest rooftop to keep watch for any of the governor's guards. They waited expectantly for their savior's arrival.

Their eagerness prompted Tabia to stand tall in the felucca as the rigging of the lateen sail creaked overhead. She immediately began to proclaim that the great god of cats called all felines her own.

"If canines persecute you for proclaiming that felines are first and foremost in the purr of Bastet-Net, do not fear," she purred. "You have nine lives! Let go of one; find another."

The crowd of felines could not risk the sound of clapping, so they padded their paws on the earth and softly miaowed, "More. Tell us more."

"Do not cower before the bully," Tabia miaowed as quietly as she could. "Do not cringe before the canine who seeks to devour you. Prowl! Stalk! Yowl! Use the gifts Bastet-Net gave you. You have nine lives!"

As sun dawned, all the felines gathered on the shore watched Tabia set sail again. With the wind behind them, she and her companions drifted around a bend of the river. They left behind contented felines, purring their belief in nine lives.

But other creatures also stood watching the boat drift away. Two canines, one jackal, three crocodiles, a single hippopotamus, and four ibis had met Tabia that night. They had begged forgiveness for how their ancestors had mistreated felines.

Yelping, bellowing, whooping, and harrumphing, they beseeched Bastet-Net to heal them of their broken wings and tusks, bloated bellies and unsightly humps, tattered ears and drooping tails.

Seeing their need, Tabia had prayed.

Bastet-Net,
> *You who created these canines and crocodiles,*
> *this jackal and hippopotamus,*
> *these ibises,*
> *remember that they, too, praise You!*

They know that You are
> *the great god of all creatures!*

Hearing this prayer, Bastet-Net had healed each of those eleven suppliants. Resolving to treat all cats fairly, they returned joyfully to their homes.

Tabia and her companions continued up the Nile to Abydos where her younger brothers and sisters crowded the shore.

"Mother is dead!" they wailed. "A Saluki guard snapped her neck because she sampled a sardine before handing over the coins to the crocodile merchant!"

Twitching her whiskers, Tabia flattened her ears and yowled, "Come! Our mother is not dead!"

Cautiously, she led her family and her companions to the necropolis in the desert that bordered Abydos. Finding her mother's resting place, Tabia prayed once again.

Nine lives have we, O Great God of Cats!
I beseech You then
    to give another life to my mother!
All praise and glory be Yours!

A dazzle of light danced across the sky. The companions gathered by the grave watched in amazement as it descended like sun rippling water. Far to the northeast, it lit the horizon.

"There, my brothers and sisters," murmured Tabia, "there is our mother! She has come back to us and is living another life somewhere here in Egypt!"

"You are sure?"

"As sure as I am that Bastet-Net purred us all!"

Rejoicing, Tabia, her family, and her companions returned to Abydos where they feasted on smoked herring, slivered vole, and goat's milk.

Chapter 13
A Judge Silences Tabia

That night, Tabia and her companions slept in Abydos as a stealthy contingent of canines quietly padded into the town. With nary a sound, they arrested her for sedition, dragged her to nearby Thebes, and tossed her into prison. Her companions woke to find her gone.

For many naps, Tabia languished in a dark cell with no window. Deprived of sunlight, she spent her days reciting the commands of Bastet-Net. In the third week of her captivity, a guard flung open the door to Tabia's cell.

"Get up," he growled. "Your trial's today. I hope you're sentenced to death!"

The guard caught hold of Tabia's tail and dragged her before Judge Gahiji. Everyone knew the judge hated cats. This hatred made reading The Theban Times an ordeal for him because of the stories he found there.

A hippopotamus who favored felines owned the newspaper. It often carried reports of feline exploits as well as stories of canine brutality toward feline demonstrators.

Reading these articles brought on Judge Gahiji's asthma attacks. Often he came to court hacking and barking. He cursed the felines who'd caused his malady.

On the morning of Tabia's trial, everyone gathered in the courtroom knew she stood little chance of acquittal in Gahiji's courtroom.

The trial went quickly. The mastiff prosecutor brought forth five key witnesses—two canines, one crocodile, one snake, and one jackal. The canines testified first.

"Who better deserves nine lives than we canines?" the first hound howled. "Wasn't it Runihura, the great alpha, who freed us from feline dominance? With such a warrior as part of our race, why would felines, and not we canines, have nine lives?"

He glared at the other creatures gathered in the courtroom and recognized that many there agreed with him. To end his testimony, he barked loudly, "Tabia has slandered our name and lied to her companions!"

The second canine was also loud in his denunciation of Tabia. "She came to Memphis and somehow conjured up a new tail for one of my workers. It was trickery! Chicanery and trickery!"

Upon further questioning, the dog, his coat smelling of dung, yapped that Tabia had then convinced the worker to open his own hairball shop. "I was left with nothing!" he whined, frothing at the mouth. "I'm begging from the very tourists who buy from her. For that alone, this bothersome feline deserves death."

Hearing this, everyone in the courtroom, with the exception of the felines, voiced cacophonous agreement.

Not to be outdone by two surly canines, Sobek, a crocodile from Tabia's birthplace, testified. "In her early years, this wicked cat welcomed every feline stray who wandered into Abydos. She showed no shame in her lewd caterwauling and wanton behavior."

Once again, the creatures gathered in the lower level of the courtroom cried out. Their shrieks of disgust reverberated throughout the chamber, but the felines in the upper reaches muttered their disgust. Who was this sanctimonious crocodile whose yellowed fourth tooth, on each side of his noisy snout, protruded upward beyond the bounds of common decency?

The final two witnesses for the prosecution related their fear of Tabia's yowls. "It's a disaster waiting to happen," the snake insisted. "When felines hear her yowl, they erupt into a mighty din. They lose themselves in an ecstasy of good mews about nine lives."

Hissing his disdain, he continued, "In their dance of rapture, those foolish felines have almost trampled me several times!"

The jackal feared that Tabia's yowl would persuade the felines of Egypt to revolt. "We've lived with them in peace now for many years," he snarled. "This upstart from Abydos wants all other creatures to revere felines, to display a suitable awe before them. What nonsense! That will lead to only one thing—feline domination again."

*   *   *

The cats in the gallery, hearing such lies about Tabia, scoffed. Their dissonance filled the courtroom. Only when the judge threatened to boil them all in oil did they cease their caterwauling. Still, many continued to murmur their loathing for him as well as for the jackal who had just testified.

Enraged, Judge Gahiji instructed the guards to bind and gag any cat obstinate enough to rumble complaint. Silence descended on the courtroom.

Next, Tabia's defense attorney—appointed by the court—stood up. He had studied at the best law school in Athens. Throughout Egypt, he was renowned as a feline who frequently won his cases even when they were tried before a canine judge.

All the creatures in the courtroom watched avidly as the defense attorney's first witness came to the stand. Mavie had sailed all the way from Wales to testify in Tabia's behalf. With great dignity, she related how she'd been possessed by canine demons.

Hearing her testimony, the canines and jackals in the courtroom shouted, "She lies! She lies!" while the crocodiles bellowed disgust and the falcons, perched on the gallery railing, keened derision.

The gallery cats immediately complained that the judge had not permitted such an outburst after the testimony of the prosecution's witnesses. Judge Gahiji, of course, ignored them.

He then growled, "No more. We need no more proof of Tabia's contempt for our canine ways. I have listened to proof of her promiscuous past and her mischief-making present. Now I am ready to pass judgment."

"But, your honor," the feline defense attorney yowled, "my second witness is a hound. His testimony will prove that Tabia is innocent of any wrongdoing."

"Who might this canine be?" the judge barked.

"Someone Tabia healed in Memphis."

"Enough. I've heard enough. Nine lives!" the judge growled. "Nine lives. And all for felines!"

The judge immediately sentenced Tabia to death by drowning.

With a loud bay of approval, the canine contingent that had arrested Tabia dragged her to the Nile. Jeering, they held her under its muddy water until her dream of life escaped and sheltered itself in Bastet-Net.

Her companions, wailing their grief, watched as Tabia's body floated down the Nile. With great hope, they announced, "She'll find another life and return to us!"

In the days that followed, no one spoke of the birth of an extraordinary cat throughout Egypt. So Sabah, the first companion of Tabia, concluded that Tabia had probably decided to spend her second life in nearby Abyssinia, wearing a stylish ruddy coat with black ticking.

"Someone has to tell the royal family of felines there that Bastet-Net has given them nine lives," Sabah miaowed. "Who better than Tabia?"

Chapter 14
Tabia's Companions Depart Thebes

After her death, Tabia's companions napped for many days. They woke, lonely for her, only to nap again. Finally, Bastet-Net purred a dream to Sabah. She awakened the others and recounted the dream to them.

"I stood on a wharf in Alexandria," Sabah purred, "watching canines load wheat, papyrus scrolls, and jars of pickled finch onto a sailing ship. All were mute. Then, suddenly, all was sound. Purrs and yowls swirled in and about, above and below me."

"What happened next?" Tabia's companions asked.

"All around me, felines of every stripe, ticking, heft, and color beckoned me east and west, north and south. Then I heard the deep rumble of Bastet-Net's purr."

"What did she say?"

In a resounding yowl, Sabah quoted Bastet-Net's message.

Go now, you companions of Tabia!

Proclaim the good mews of nine lives!

Tell every feline that for nine lives
they can nap, hunt, prowl!
For nine lives, they can rest securely
within my dream!

Trek to Tibet and China.
Sail to Syria and Rome.
Pad to every land where felines dwell!
Proclaim my gift!

This command from Bastet-Net bemused Tabia's companions. Mesmerized, they listened as Sabah shared more of her dream.

"I saw canine sailors beckoning me. 'Come,' they shouted. 'Other lands await you!' The wind moved suddenly through me, lifting me skyward and carrying me onto the ship. I yowled good-bye to Egypt and set sail!"

Sabah gazed steadily at Tabia's companions, who sat enraptured by her dream. Again and again they beseeched her to recount its details. She did so. Always at the end, she encouraged them to leave Thebes, the place where their leader had yielded her first life.

"Let us carry the good mews of nine lives to lands beyond our ken," she purred. "Let us slumber in forest, field, and village. Between our napping and our eating, let us proclaim Bastet-Net's gift of nine lives!"

So Tabia's companions departed Egypt, none knowing whether they would ever again groom one another. Sabah, the first to leave, sailed down river to Alexandria. She boarded a trading ship, crossed the Great Sea, and landed on the island of Corsica.

The next day, she embarked on a second ship to cross the channel to Italy. Regrettably, the felines in Rome found her mews only moderately interesting, so Sabah continued north where many cats gleefully accepted their gift of nine lives.

Sabah spent the next five years in the northern climes. Never again did she return to Thebes. In southern Gaul, a mob of enraged bears, angry because she had nine lives while they had only one, roasted her over a crackling cedar fire. No one knows where Sabah spent her second life.

* * *

Other companions of Tabia also left Egypt, trekking to foreign lands. Second to sail was Hadi. Before departing, he paid his debts to the fish merchants in Alexandria and Memphis. Then he sailed the Nile upriver to where the Abbai joined it. Carefully, he steered his felucca eastward and traveled to where the river rose in the highlands of Abyssinia.

There he docked at a village along the shore and announced the great gift Bastet-Net had given all felines. The local canine authorities jeered and trotted back to the garrison.

"What does a foreign cat know about life?" they muttered to one another.

"Probably slinking away from the governor in Egypt!" the head guard woofed. "We'll have to check."

Hadi spent the season of flood in the village, but left when the yearly drought draped the land. During his stay, only a few cats came to believe in the good mews of nine lives. Nightly, those who did danced while yowling their song of deliverance.

> *Praise Bastet-Net.*
>
> *We have nine lives.*
>
> *Let us cease our cowering*
> *before accursed canines.*
>
> *For what is death*
> *but entry into another life?*

For eleven years, Hadi padded over Abyssinia, hoping always to meet Tabia in her second life. Miracles followed Hadi's paw prints. Always he beseeched Bastet-Net to graciously perform these mighty deeds. So it was that one day his prayer healed a street cleaner who had cut her paws on shards of littered glass.

The scruffy feline, unable to do her cleaning, feared that the vizier would fire her.

"What will I do then?" she wailed. "He will toss me out of my dustbin. How will I eat? I cannot hunt with these shredded paws."

"Do you trust Bastet-Net?" Hadi asked.

"I do!"

"Then beseech her. Your paws will heal so that once again you can pad regally throughout this city."

Together, the two entreated Bastet-Net for healing. Together they praised her as the wounds on the street cleaner's paws sealed themselves into health. Great was Bastet-Net!

As crescent moons came and went, Hadi longed to see his home once again. Weariness had burrowed deep within his bones; his joints creaked with age.

When he could no longer withstand his longing, Hadi departed Abyssinia and sailed back down the Abbai to the Nile. Often he napped under the lateen sail of his shallow-draft boat as it drifted downstream. Only when he came to Thebes did Hadi rise from the bottom of the felucca.

Rumbling a deep purr, he joined his wife in front of the hut where she had dwelt long years without him. For nine days, she scolded Hadi for his desertion. But when he told her of all he'd endured, she welcomed him home and they entered their one-room hut together.

Within his home, Hadi settled on the fireside mat from which he never rose again. Soon after that, Bastet-Net called him into her presence. Together they curve their sleek bodies around a dream of grace and beauty.

*   *   *

Like Sabah and Hadi, most of Tabia's companions went out into the world to proclaim that Bastet-Net had given felines nine lives. However, Widjan stayed in Egypt. Tabia's companions had selected her to be the first high feline of the great god of cats.

Widjan settled along the Nile at the temple of Bastet-Net. There, she yowled the good mews of nine lives to all felines who came to praise the great god of cats.

With each full moon, Widjan felt the ecstasy of the great god's grace. Her yowl echoed against the tall columns of the temple and reverberated throughout the valley of the great river. Thus it was that at each full moon, she lost herself within the dream of Bastet-Net.

Chapter 15
Tabia's Companions Travel Far and Wide

Among those companions who did leave Egypt, several—besides Sabah and Hadi—deserve mention. One padded to Syria. There he died after serving a royal canine family of Salukis for many years.

Daily he had diligently prepared meals and padded to the bin with trash. When not doing this, he went out into the marketplace to announce Bastet-Net's gift to passing felines. The Salukis allowed him to do this because he had healed their son of mange.

Another of Tabia's companions, taking only his coat and a staff, trekked westward across the desert. There he suffocated in a windstorm before he could tell the nomadic felines, who pitched their tents on the vast sands, that Bastet-Net had given them nine lives.

A third companion climbed the remote mountains of Tibet only to be crucified by the ruling mastiffs who feared her message. A fourth, ever faithful to Bastet-Net's gift, sailed beyond the Great Sea to the isle of Britain. There miracles accompanied the swish of his tail, the twitch of his whiskers.

A fourth companion—Lisimba—crossed the Great Sea and brought the good mews of nine lives to felines in

Greece. Daily, he roared the good mews to feline Stoics when they assembled on the Pynx in Athens.

On this rocky elevation, Lisimba proclaimed the advantages of Bastet-Net's gift of nine lives. However, the feline Stoics had put aside a longing for the future and simply purred contentedly in their present.

"We do not indulge in whimsy," one Stoic yawned. "We honor all creatures who work for justice. All Stoics—be they canine or fox, wolf or jackal, eagle or snake—are happy in this life because they practice virtue."

A second feline Stoic purred, "That must please Bastet-Net more than the constant insipid mewling of frenzied felines!"

Given this attitude, Lisimba had little success in Greece. Disappointed, but not dispirited, he sailed from the port of Piraeus and landed in Spain. There, he rove the mountains, imparting his good mews of nine lives to any feline peasant he met. For five years, these grateful cats hid Lisimba from marauding canines who sought to silence him.

In the Spanish mountains, Lisimba breathed his last, as age and infirmity captured him. "This has been a wonderful life," he miaowed. "The second will be even better!"

With a final purr of content, he died.

*   *   *

Alima—a youthful companion of Tabia's—also tried to carry Bastet-Net's good mews of nine lives to Spain, but a torrential storm capsized the ship on which she sailed. A strong undercurrent sucked Alima into the depths of the Great Sea as she yowled, "All praise to Bastet-Net!"

The waters claimed Alima, but even as she drowned she trusted that another life awaited her.

After hearing Sabah's dream, Jala, another of Tabia's companions, slung her traveling bag over her shoulders, then crossed the eastern desert. Within a fortnight, the cats who lived on the steppes slumbered in ease—Bastet-Net's gift had freed them from their fear of the local sheik.

Day after day, this harsh canine had sent them out into the arid desert to hunt for agates, jasper, and amethyst. They were too tired to praise Bastet-Net when they returned each night with their sacks of precious stones.

Jala told these weary slaves about the gift of the great god of cats. Hearing this mews, one feline on the sunbaked mountains that lay along the Red Sea, yowled, "No longer will I work all day for this canine sheik. If he refuses me my nap, I'll refuse to work. He'll surely cut me into pieces and feed me to the falcons, but I'll have another life!"

The next day, forty fearless felines marched into the shadowy tent of the sheik, demanding their rights. He denounced their intrusion, but they insisted on change.

"No longer will we work long hours with no nap or snooze," they yowled. "One hour will we work in that desert sun. One hour and no longer!"

Yelping dismay, the sheik commanded his minions to bind the cats' paws and pitch them out into the desert. All through the day, the sun roasted them. At sunset, when the guards sniffed the limp bodies, only twenty-five still lived, but they refused to work more than one hour the next day.

Again, the sheik cast them into the desert. By the end of that second day, eight more felines had died and gone to their next life.

Now the sheik reconsidered. With his work force depleted, perhaps seventeen felines working one hour a day was better than none. Thus did the gift of Bastet-Net free these felines.

* * *

Thabit, an intrepid follower of Tabia, crossed the Great Sea to Asia Minor. From there he climbed cloud-ringed mountains and descended verdant valleys until he came to the Caspian Sea. Crossing over, he arrived in Scythia where he met half-wild cats who knew nothing of Bastet-Net and her commands.

From dusk to dawn, Thabit related his memories of Tabia and gave to the Scythian cats the message of Bastet-Net's great gift. As they began to accept her commands, their scruffy fur became sleek and their gaze calm.

Thabit also taught the felines of Scythia to farm. He sent messages back to Egypt, beseeching felines artisans there to come to Scythia to teach paw printing and the art of hairball tapestries.

In Thabit's lifetime, the Scythia felines became prosperous and began to trade with merchant cats in Italy, Britain, Egypt, Judaea, Syria, and Gaul.

Throughout this heathen land, Thabit set up schools, not only for felines but for all creatures who lived there. Teachers came from throughout the Canine Empire to instruct the students in the fine arts of civilization. Thus, besides the good mews of nine lives, Thabit brought culture—the gift of felines—to Scythia.

* * *

One final pupil of Tabia deserves attention. Fatin left Thebes and padded to Babylon, a city infamous for its feline slavery. There, cloaked in a flowing robe, she captivated the canine governor.

From the spacious pockets of that robe, this enterprising feline pulled cooing mourning doves. Within an ear's twitch, they flew upward, built nests, and laid eggs. Within a tail's wag, chicks hatched, joining their coos to the doves' song.

Butterflies fluttered to the ceilings from the collar of Fatin's robe. Their bright wings quivered in the breeze wafting from the open windows.

Red flowers sprouted from the buttons of his robe. Crimson beams of light shone from within and without these blooms. The governor chortled in glee when their light illuminated his throne room.

"You're a magician! Come! Do more magic!"

Fatin bowed. Rising, he miaowed, "This magic is as nothing to the mews I bring the felines in Babylon."

"Mews for felines, but not for me?"

"For you, too! My mews is that Bastet-Net has gifted felines with nine lives."

"I see," the governor woofed, "how that is good for them. But what is the gift to me?"

"Ah!" Fatin smiled. "If felines live nine lives, think how long they may serve you and your cohorts!"

Of course, this cunning messenger of good mews was only trying to trick the governor. Fatin was sure that if the Babylonian felines chose to live nine lives, they'd settle elsewhere after each death. Why endure the slavery of this unenlightened city in Mesopotamia?

The governor—enthralled with the prospect of long years of feline servitude—allowed Fatin to announce her message day and night to the Babylonian cats.

He permitted them to leave their work—be it as clerk or farmer, apothecary or glassblower, woodcutter or smith, peddler or lawyer, hairballist or street cleaner—and gather at dusk to listen to her message.

All the felines in Babylon welcomed this mews. Nine lives! And they had to live only one in Babylon!

Chapter 16
Omar Encounters Mystery

One last feline carried the good mews of nine lives to the ancient world. Omar came late to his belief in Bastet-Net's gift. He came late and then yowled loud and long. His background was of interest to many felines once he began to proclaim the good mews.

Omar grew up in Nubia where his father was head of a fine school for cats. From Omar's father, the kits of Nubia learned about the canine revolution led by Runihura. He also explained to them how the governor of Malta had convinced Runihura to call a truce in which canines wielded all power, but lived in peace with cats.

As Omar grew older, he realized that his father was mired in the past. Clearly, the future lay with canines.

For many moons, he watched the soldiers who guarded his hometown. Omar, an admirer of ostentation, longed to wear their uniforms: bronze greaves, figured breastplates, and helmets bedecked with ostrich plumes. He, too, wanted to patrol their city and capture those who refused to obey the law—be they canine, crocodile, or even cat!

Wearied of being only a learned feline, Omar left his father's home and sought work as a defender of peace. For three years, he served the canine governor of Nubia, clawing his way up to become his aide.

As time passed, the governor came to rely on Omar's shrewdness as he dealt with these obstinate felines. Omar became the governor's most trusted spy. Daily, this ambitious cat slunk among feline carousers, his ears perked for boasts about feline uniqueness and grumbles of discontent.

Omar was able to arrest many of these cats and toss them into prison. He'd torture those who refused to acknowledge that canines had the right to rule.

Ashamed, Omar's father padded to the prison to disown his son's deeds. "You do not honor the ancient ways!" he complained.

But Omar had only contempt for felines who resisted the alpha of the Canine Empire. He found these cats ignorant, for they refused to accept that canines would, forevermore, rule their lives.

As summer edged its way into autumn, the governor heard rumors about a group of cats who lived in hermitages by the Red Sea. He immediately summoned his spy Omar.

"They dance and clap! They're making a genuine nuisance of themselves!" the governor woofed.

He shared with his spy all he knew of this group of recalcitrant felines. He barked the story of how the ruler of Egypt had executed a cat there named Tabia.

"According to her accursed companions, this Tabia," the governor scoffed, "now lives a second life in Abyssinia! And why did the governor of Egypt execute her?"

The governor did not wait for Omar to try to guess. Instead, he snarled, "Why? Why? I'll tell you why! Because she maintained that cats have nine lives! Supposedly that's why they celebrate at each new moon. To thank Bastet-Net."

The Nubian governor, fearing that these refractory felines would catapult others into insurrection, ordered Omar to disband the group.

The governor's lackey, ever practical, was pleased to serve him. Why not? Such moonstruck cats brought only disgrace on others. Or so Omar reasoned.

The next day, he set out eastward to the sunbaked, arid deserts bordering the Red Sea. The farther he went, the more he bristled with indignation at cats who dared insist that they had nine lives. How ridiculous! Once again, they were bringing down the wrath of canines onto cats everywhere.

"One bad feline spoils the whole clowder," he yowled.

As Omar trekked toward the Red Sea, he vowed to arrest the obstinate cats and drag them back to the capital city of Nubia. He'd imprison them in cells with no cushions or hidey-holes for their napping. No dozing in comfort.

Omar vowed to strew the floor with shards of glass, annoying burrs, and prickly thistles. He'd shutter the windows so they couldn't bask in the sun's warmth.

* * *

The harvest moon was rising in the eastern sky when Omar arrived at the first feline hermitage. Battering the door, he prepared to arrest the inhabitants within. He opened his mouth to yowl a command, but his throat issued no sound!

Purr, miaow, mewl, and even yowl deserted him!

Omar stood mute before the aged cat who finally opened the door. Again and again Omar tried to speak—but his voice had abandoned him. Nor could he hear the felines crowded into the derelict hermitage.

Mute, deaf, befuddled, he dropped his sword to the ground. The ears of each cat within the room twitched; their whiskers quivered; their mouths moved. Omar heard nothing.

As if in a dream, he watched as all gathered within the shack beckoned him to enter. All around him, color and shape swirled so that he felt himself sinking into a soundless whorl that spiraled to the heavens and into the depths of earth. He floated within a chasm of void.

The bemused felines led him to a mat. After removing his bronze breastplate, helmet, and greaves, they pulled a blanket over his shivering body. The only sound in the room was that of his chattering teeth.

None of those felines gathered in that ramshackle hut knew that Omar felt himself caught within a circle that spun in a haze of sun, a mist of rain, a torment of thunder, a splinter of lightning.

For three days, Omar lay deaf and mute on that pallet. Yet threaded within his slumber was the purr of Bastet-Net.

Omar, I am Nine Lives!

Do not fear this good mews of my gift!

You, too, I have blessed with nine lives!

I want you to carry mews of my gift
to felines throughout the world!

Rejoice!

Omar had thought he knew and understood Bastet-Net. But during this time, he realized he knew nothing. Her yowl became presence in the marrow of his being. Her miaow became his sustenance. Her purr became his silent praise.

On the third day of his stupor, Omar rose from the mat, stretched his lithe body, twitched his whiskers, licked his paws, and yowled, "I have nine lives! It is Bastet-Net's gift to me!"

The felines gathered in that hut by the Red Sea lifted their wedged heads and praised Bastet-Net. "Cateluia! Cateluia! Cateluia!"

For nine full moons, Omar dwelt by the shore of the Red Sea. Day and night, he mused. From dawn to dusk, he praised the great god of cats. From dusk to dawn, he sat with the felines of the Red Sea to hear the story of how Tabia had announced Bastet-Net's gift of nine lives.

As the tenth full moon strode the sky, Omar purred good-bye to the felines of the Red Sea. Leaving the hermitage behind, he vowed to tell all cats in the known world that Bastet-Net had given them the gift of nine lives.

To begin his mission, Omar first journeyed westward to Egypt to find the first companions of Tabia. From them he hoped to learn the height and depth, the length and width, the ins and outs, the above and below, the within and without, the seen and unseen of what Tabia had known of Bastet-Net.

Chapter 17
Omar Yowls the Good Mews

Omar, who once eagerly served the canine governor of Nubia, now longed to serve only Bastet-Net. For seven years, he sailed the Great Sea, even journeying as far as Spain. Eagerly, he traveled the deserts of Egypt to Mauretania.

He ambled across Judaea, the Galilee, and Syria, then turned toward Parthia. He traveled with tail erect, its tip stiff and upright. Thus did he greet the felines he met.

In each city or village he entered, he went to the highest place and yowled his good mews. But Omar utilized more than his voice. He had perfected the use of his tail.

So, for instance, he curved it gently down to purr the story of Tabia's birth. He held his tail erect, its tip tilted over, when he wanted felines to listen and accept the good mews of nine lives. Seeing this, some cats perked their tufted ears and settled themselves on the flagstoned streets.

Most cats, however, found his mews only mildly interesting. In the middle of one of his long harangues about the life of Tabia, many simply dozed.

Often they awakened to find him still yowling— hoarsely. It was then they'd beg, "Tell us something that will make our lives better now. Let us reign again!"

Omar endeavored to win their attention by telling stories about the ancient prophets. Despite the drama of these stories, most felines simply ignored him. They'd stretch, yawn widely, and fall into a deep sleep.

Others insisted on yowling their disdain for his message. "We want a life of ease again! It is ours by right for we are awesome beings!" They simply closed their ears to the good mews that Tabia had sung. They saw no possibilities in it.

*   *   *

Despite these setbacks, Omar never wearied of praising the great god of cats. He grew gaunt trudging over the roads into the hinterlands of Parthia and Scythia, Armenia, and Asia Minor. He seldom napped but spent all his time trying to convince lazy felines that Bastet-Net had given them a great gift.

His journey brought many hardships. In Mesopotamia, the canine governor imprisoned him. With great fortitude, throughout each day and night in his dark dungeon, Omar yowled his song of belief in nine lives.

When the next harvest moon rose, Omar predicted to his cellmates—three mice who had been caught stealing grain—that a great tremor would move the earth that night.

"The earth waits to tremble on the command of Bastet-Net," he miaowed. "We'll be free before dawn!"

As the mice slept, Omar prayed to Bastet-Net to deliver him from captivity. And so it was. When night was deep in slumber, a mighty quake shook the earth.

The walls of all the houses crumbled into dust. Canines, donkeys, sheep, falcons, salamanders—all creatures there—rushed to find shelter beyond the town.

Suddenly the door of his cell sprung open. Omar yowled, "Come! We're free!"

Despite his encouragement, the three mice refused to follow for fear of what the canine guards would do should they be recaptured. Omar himself strode forth into the night, sighing at such timidity. He took up again his journey to spread the good mews of Bastet-Net far and wide.

Guards in other villages, towns, and cities also arrested Omar, but no cell could contain the astounding mews of the great god's gift. Always, Bastet-Net or Omar's own cajolery brought freedom. Always he lived to nap another day.

It was in Syria that Bastet-Net called Omar to curve himself into her dream. The canine governor there feared that the troublesome feline would incite his subjects to rebel. So the mastiff sent guards to arrest Omar.

The next day, the governor boiled him alive in a huge cauldron set in the city square.

* * *

Word of this soon reached Widjan, the first high feline of Bastet-Net. Fervently, she thanked the great god of cats for Omar.

"Praise to Bastet-Net who purred Omar into a dream that took him into the wilderness of the Canine Empire," Widjan purred. "All felines will honor his name forevermore! May he nap with the great god of cats until time folds itself into her dream."

Thus ended the forays of Tabia's companions. They announced her astonishing good mews of nine lives to felines throughout the Canine Empire and beyond. They napped beneath the sun in every country. They snoozed into the dream of Bastet-Net.

Cateluia! Cateluia! Cateluia!

And may all canines pad carefully for only cats have nine lives!

Other Books by Dee Ready

A Cat's Life: Dulcy's Story
Available in paperback and ebook formats.

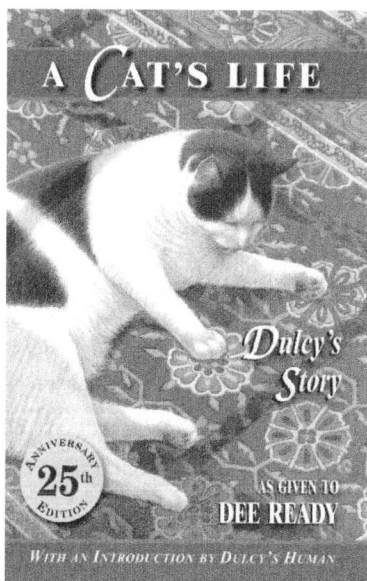

A Cat's Life: Dulcy's Story—On a late winter's day in 1972, a kitten soon to be named Dulcy found a woman worthy to be her human. For the next 17 years, Dulcy and her human learned to communicate on a level deeper than language and to comfort one another with affectionate routines that softened the shocks of an inconstant world.

A Cat's Legacy:
Dulcy's Companion Book
Available in paperback and ebook formats.

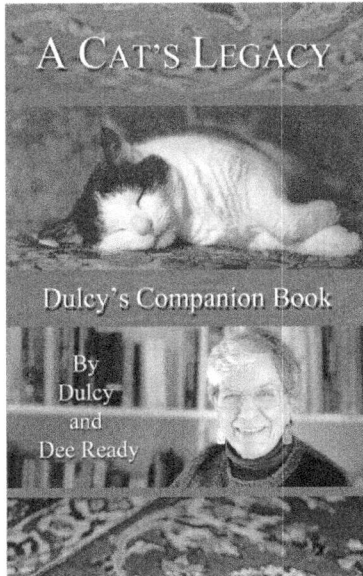

A Cat's Legacy: Dulcy's Companion Book—In her second book, Dulcy shares stories about twelve habits she perfected while living with her human. When followed, these habits assure bliss in any relationship. For each habit, Dee—Dulcy's human—explains how the habit also influenced her life. These stories speak to all cat lovers who delight in the foibles of their feline companions.

Prayer Wasn't Enough
A Convent Memoir
Available in paperback and ebook formats.

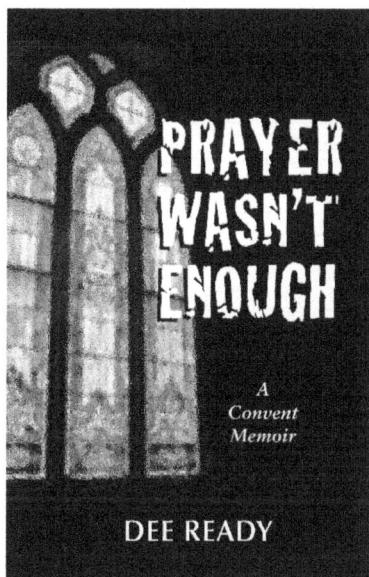

In 1958, Dee Ready entered a Benedictine convent, certain that there she'd become a saint. As Sister Innocence, she prayed, taught, and stumbled over her own clay feet. Years later she left the convent, certain she was a fraud.

In this convent memoir, an ex-nun describes the crippling hunger for perfection, flawed misconception of sanctity, and emotional immaturity she brought to religious life. Her story appeals to those whose dreams for the future have been shaken or derailed.

Upcoming Novel by Dee Ready

The Reluctant Spy

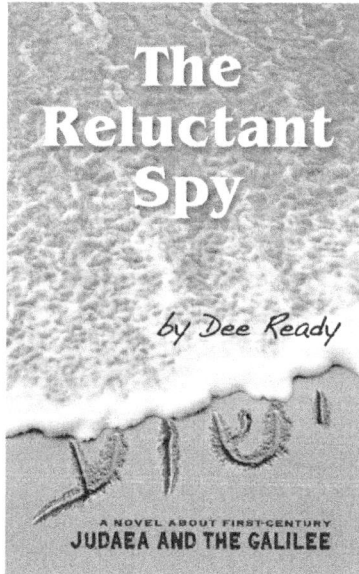

Pressured into spying on Yeshua (often called Jesus), Jonathan, a village scribe, reluctantly travels to the Galilee. With growing envy, he observes Yeshua—an itinerant rabbi and exorcist. Hounded by a crisis of faith, Jonathan now faces its consequences. How far has he fled from the God who pursues him? Is he able to accept Yeshua's belief in him? When factions in Jerusalem collide and tragic events ensue, is Jonathan able to believe in himself?

Available soon.

About the Author

Dulcy's human, Dee Ready, lives in Independence, Missouri, with three cats: Ellie, Maggie, and Matthew. When not playing with them, she blogs, works on the craft of writing, and enjoys exploring the mysterious world of felines. With the help of Dulcy, she has written *A Cat's Life: Dulcy's Story* (Book 1) and *A Cat's Legacy: Dulcy's Companion Book* (Book 2). Dee's latest publication is the convent memoir *Prayer Wasn't Enough.*

Find Dee Ready Online

Website: www.DeeReady.com

Facebook: www.facebook.com/DeeReadyaspiringnovelist

Blog: cominghometomyself.blogspot.com

Twitter: @dee_ready36

Made in the USA
Coppell, TX
07 January 2021

47485756R00075